The Curse of Jean Lafitte

Mary Walsh

The Big Easy Collection, Book 2

Discover other titles by Mary Walsh

American Posse

Knights of the Corporate Round Table

Memories of 9/11

Plenty of Fish in the Ocean State

Once Upon a Time in Chicago

His Second Chance

Life Lessons for My Kids

Wounded but not Dead

Fine Spirits Served Here

Stable of Studs

Where or When

Catch a Break

Dragon Slayer

You Deserve Better

Acknowledgments

Even though I live in Pennsylvania, New Orleans is one of my favorite cities. But not because of drinking and partying on Bourbon Street. Honestly, I avoid that scene after dark. There's so much more to do in the French Quarter and surrounding neighborhoods - listen to live jazz, eat jambalaya in top-notch restaurants, join a wedding parade as it marches down the street. The energy and romanticism fill me every time I go.

In June 2022, I did a Meet the Author Event at world-famous Antoine's Restaurant for my book *Fine Spirits Served Here* and met some fabulous people. While I was there, I connected with Paige Vance. Like me, she is originally a Yankee and moved to New Orleans in 2014. Paige and I spent an hour and a half on a video call one winter night as she described the ins and outs of being a transplant in her new adopted city. As she talked, I took pages and pages of notes. What better way to get inside information than from a local!

My editor, Ingrid Edisen, is also from Louisiana. She used to live in New Orleans, but now makes Lafayette her home. Aside from giving me amazing critiques and ideas to make all of my books better, she gave me insight into the 'right' things about living in New Orleans. She corrected this Yankee several times: It's *on* the neutral ground, not *at* the neutral ground. The Mississippi runs low in October, so it's *not* flooding season. And you only eat oysters in months that contain "r." After reading *Fine Spirits Served Here,* Ingrid was impressed with how well I portrayed the character of New Orleans without ever having lived there. She challenged me to do another novel set in the city and that's how this book was born.

Roberta at Keil's Antiques on Royal Street needs a shout-out. I met her for the first time in October 2021 when I gave her a copy of *Fine Spirits Served Here.* In that book, a character is based on a real-life porter, Bennie Hensley, who worked at Keil's for almost 80 years. Roberta asked me if I wanted to see Bennie and I said sure! Expecting a portrait, I followed Roberta to a corner of the shop only to find a small marble box on the floor. The urn contained Bennie's ashes so that he could always stay at the store. I thought to myself, *Only in New Orleans!*

Several staff members at Lafitte's Blacksmith Shop Bar took time out of their busy day to talk to me as I did research for this book. Shelly, Bree, and Harrison: I can't thank you enough.

To my dear friend and mentor, Bruce Mowday, you are Master Yoda to my Princess Leia.

The cover for this book was hand painted by my friend Mike Weber. He is a software developer by day and a talented artist by night. After I went back and forth on several ideas for a title, Mike's wife, Meredith, convinced me to use The Curse of Jean Lafitte.

Lastly, my husband, Dave, has supported my writing from the day he met me and knows to not interrupt me when I'm nose deep in my laptop working on a scene. My wonderful husband was on board when I bought a pricey chandelier from Fischer-Gambino on Royal Street. It hangs in our dining room on the west side of the house. Every evening, when the sun sets, hundreds of rainbow prisms light up the room. Dave teases me that he'll someday spread my ashes in New Orleans. Thank you for being my number one fan.

There are so many more people to thank for this book. You know who you are. My support system has been amazing. I am forever grateful to all of you.

Here's a Big Easy playlist to help get you in the mood:

- Down in New Orleans - Dr. John
- House Of The Rising Sun - The Animals
- Born on the Bayou - Creedence Clearwater Revival
- I Wish I Was In New Orleans - Tom Waits
- Tremé Song - John Boutté
- Do You Know What It Means To Miss New Orleans? - Billie Holiday and Louis Armstrong
- Oh, My NOLA - Harry Connick, Jr.
- Where Y'at - Trombone Shorty
- New Orleans Shout - Bourbon Street Jazzband

My favorite things to do in New Orleans:

- Ride a streetcar (it's streetcar, not trolley, unless you want the locals to look at you funny)
- Go to Rouses Market to get Creole and Cajun spices. The River Road brand is my favorite.
- Head out early in the morning for a stroll through the French Quarter. No one is out at 7:00 except for shopkeepers and restaurant owners opening up for the day. The sidewalks are empty and you can smell the fig and orange trees.
- Listen to live jazz at Fritzel's. During the day, Harold the bartender makes a mean hurricane.
- Go on a ghost tour. Are ghosts real? Who knows. But I've captured 'questionable' things in my pictures.

My favorite restaurants:

- Dooky Chase

  2301 Orleans Ave, Tremé

  I can't say enough about this restaurant. The staff! The food! The ambiance! Leah Chase took pride in her eating house and you can tell.

- Horn's Eatery

  2440 Chartres St, Marigny

  I first stumbled upon this bungalow café on my way to a Little Free Library. I asked for an iced tea to go and they didn't charge me. On my second trip, I stayed for breakfast and dined among the locals at this hidden gem. I was happy it wasn't overloaded with tourists.

- Majoria's Commerce

  300 Camp St, Central Business District

  This diner is only open for breakfast and lunch. It's a small and crowded place so get here early, otherwise you might be waiting on the sidewalk. The servers are busy but still take great care of you. I had the half-size CBB (Commerce Breakfast Biscuit) and the server offered me a pancake on the side because pancakes aren't always available.

- New Orleans Creole Cookery

  508 Toulouse St, French Quarter

  If you want to sample a lot of the food that New Orleans is famous for, get the Taste of New Orleans: jambalaya, crawfish etouffee, shrimp creole, and red beans and rice. Delicious!

- Port of Call

  838 Esplanade Ave, on the edge of the French Quarter and the Marigny

  This 50-year-old dive bar is great for burgers and drinks. The menu is limited so don't expect many options. They do one thing and they do it well. Note: The entrance door is narrow and you need to walk up a few stairs to get to it, so it might not be good for anyone with disabilities.

- Pascal's Manale

  1838 Napoleon Ave, Freret

  This place has been around since 1913 and it's still going strong. Get their famous barbeque shrimp. The crustaceans are as big as a small child. Kidding!

- The Camellia Grille

  626 S Carrollton Ave, East Carrollton

  This small landmark diner is at the end of St. Charles Ave. If you don't have a car, the street car ride through the Garden District is a good hour or stop there on your way to/from the airport. Save room for the chocolate chip pecan pie!

I hope you enjoy this trip to The Big Easy!

Mary

October 14, 2023

Chapter 1

Halloween in New Orleans. At every corner, the locals celebrated the departed souls who built their city. And some had never left.

The spooky season in New Orleans was an unparalleled, transcendent phenomenon. While other cities carved rudimentary jack o'-lanterns and passed out fun-sized candy bars to children dressed as their favorite superheroes, New Orleans held the authority on revering the entire month of October. Most of the Halloween debauchery was celebrated on shameless Bourbon Street and flowed out into the heart of the French Quarter.

Like everything else, The City of the Dead took its favorite holiday to the extreme. A giant wooden pumpkin arched the entrance to the French Market. Tour guides donned vampire capes and top hats as they guided unsuspecting sightseers through dimly lit streets, teasing their guests into believing they would see a ghost. A clutter of costumed skeletons invaded the front lawn of a St. Charles Avenue house with taglines of "May the corpse be with you" and "BONEfied BONe Vivant." The Krewe of Boo Parade turned Vieux Carré into Boo Carré with lavish purple and orange floats the weekend before Halloween. On Royal Street, brave mortals ventured onto the sidewalk beneath LaLaurie Mansion, risking their destiny, haunted by the souls of tortured and murdered slaves.

Through the fog barely lit by the new moon of the month, *The Pride* rocked back and forth on the mighty Mississippi. The ghost ship defied Hurricane Betsy, Katrina, and, more recently, Ida. Local legend, and through the eyes of inebriated tourists, stated that the phantom vessel haunted the powerful river. No one could board and no one could leave. On calm nights, music and laughter rolled off of the ship. Her hexed crew had been patiently waiting. For two centuries, a curse had kept them on that boat jealously watching the French Quarter evolve and modernize. Their time had finally come. Now their captain, Jean Lafitte, could disembark and reverse the voodoo, releasing them of their purgatory.

A tall, thin man, Lafitte wore a long red velvet coat adorned with gold buttons that covered a gaily-colored silk shirt. Black taffeta breeches and woolen stockings protected his legs. His attire was made from the finest silk and wool that he acquired from wealthy passengers aboard captured ships. A pistol was attached to his sash with a cord so that, once fired, it could be dropped quickly but not lost while he resorted to the cutlass attached to his hip. He was gifted the gold-handled sword by his brother and business partner Pierre after they successfully assisted Andrew Jackson in the Battle of New Orleans. Fancy-buckled shoes and a black leather tricorn hat completed his look. Lafitte was the captain of *The Pride* and was expected to dress the part, even if he hadn't successfully stepped on land in two hundred years. The strumpets he bedded two centuries earlier had called him handsome and charming. He missed their company.

He stood on the quarter-deck, addressing his crew. The ragtag men were tired. Tired of waiting. Tired of each other. Tired of only having the boundary of *The Pride* as their life for the past two centuries. They desired the company of women. The debaucherous activities of the French Quarter had taunted them long enough. They had repeatedly eaten the same beans, biscuits, and salted beef and wanted to taste something new. They begged to sail on a new adventure, yearning for the open waters. Ronan the quartermaster called for all hand hoy.

"Avast ye mateys," Lafitte shouted to them, "the time has finally come!"

Cheers erupted in front of him. The men hoisted steins of grog in salute.

"The two hundredth new moon of October is nigh. I can now leave the ship without repercussions. In a fortnight, when the moon is full, we shall be free! Stay here and I shall return soon with our independence!"

More cheers echoed around the deck. Lafitte and his crew had not aged in two hundred years. The spell they were under kept them from growing old or dying while they waited on the ship. Temporary immortality had its pros and cons. They were not ghosts, but felt a special power inside them. Curses could do that.

Excited palms pounded Lafitte's back, and his crew wished him luck. His sailors' faces showed hope and pride for their captain. He climbed into the dinghy and rowed for the shore. Yelps and hurrahs echoed from the ship. Their freedom was on the horizon.

Lafitte was rarely nervous. This was one of those times. As he pushed away from *The Pride*, a ripple of panic filled him. He had been on the safety of the boat for what seemed like an eternity and now he wasn't sure what to expect. As his crew watched him, he courageously dipped his hand into the river, his fear changing to elation.

The strong pirate sat poised in the small dinghy. He was a skillful sailor. The boat gently bobbed atop the river's surface, reflecting the indigo sky above. As he gripped the oars firmly in his calloused hands, the sinewy muscles in his arms and back rippled with power. His chest expanded with each controlled breath, his focused expression revealed his determination. With a graceful rhythm, he leaned back, muscles tensing, and then propelled himself forward, sending the wooden oars slicing into the water.

The dinghy responded obediently, gliding forward with each forceful stroke. The water parted smoothly around the bow, leaving a trail of ripples in its wake. Droplets of water danced in the air as the oars emerged from the river, only to dip back in again, an intricate dance between the proud pirate and the boat. His motions were efficient, precise, and laden with controlled strength. With every pull, the boat surged forward, gathering momentum as he poured his energy into each stroke. The oars creaked softly against the wooden oarlocks, the sound a rhythmic accompaniment to the harmony of man, boat, and water. Lafitte missed that feeling.

As the distance between him and the shoreline decreased and the safety of the ship increased behind him, the pirate's focus remained unbroken.

Time would tell if this excursion was fortuitous. A small current of river water splashed onto Lafitte's dinghy. The last time one of his crew attempted to leave the ship, he was sent to Davy Jones's Locker. A bead of panicked sweat formed on Lafitte's brow. Few things frightened him. Not even the ocean or the rival buccaneers who threatened him. But the river did. The curse forced this feeling deep inside him. He gasped, knowing what could happen to him, but his fears quickly eased when the water seeped away without harm. A relieved exhale escaped his lips.

Were his eyes deceiving him? Too much time spent on the ship had affected his vision. He rubbed his eyes as he thought he saw an apparition of his ill-fated seaman Poopdeck Pete. When the younger sailor dove into the river and attempted to leave *The Pride*, the waters swallowed him whole, never to be seen again.

A few minutes later, he reached the shore. As Lafitte regained his land legs, the heels of his leather boots clapped against the river's weathered, wooden dock. The sound echoed into the night. He took two unsteady steps getting used to the solid earth, finally standing proud and erect. Being on a boat for so long affected his balance. He strode as if he owned the land upon which he walked. The transformation was almost instantaneous. Captain Jean Lafitte was back.

In a few nights, the barely viewable moon above him would soon be a slender crescent in the dark sky. The upcoming shape reminded him of the moniker that he'd heard coined in 1835 for the port city around him, The Crescent City. Like the hidden moon looking down on him, the French Quarter was built in the early 1700s at a sharp bend in the Mississippi River, mimicking the moon above. The chemistry created by the river water, egrets, and camellia blossoms permeated the air.

He made his way north along the near-empty Moonwalk Riverfront Park. Beside him, tall, black street lamps lit the path. Their ominous structure stood sentry as the gateway to landlubbers. Lafitte and his crew had watched from the ship as the lamps changed from oil-lit to electricity over the years.

A few buzzed Halloween revelers wandered by absorbed in their own fun. Lafitte left the park and crossed over the adjacent streetcar tracks. This mode of transportation remained unchanged, almost as long as he had waited to break the wretched curse.

Up and to his right, the French Market had shuttered for the night, its peddlers to return at first light. Most of the nearby buildings had maintained their original Spanish and French-style facades. He was happy that some things still looked familiar to him. Lafitte made his way through small crowds on the sidewalk. Their tacky costumes and foul language puzzled him. He couldn't tell who was Creole and who was Cajun anymore. This wasn't the same New Orleans that he knew.

Five men dressed as pirates sauntered toward him. He didn't recognize the foes and tapped a hand to his sword, ready for a duel. A few steps behind, a man in authentic royalty garments joined the group. He didn't seem to belong and no one else except Lafitte noticed him. The man caught Lafitte's eye and the two exchanged a vengeful stare. Lafitte had the feeling he knew the man, but couldn't place him. Did he cross swords with him in the middle of Jackson Square two hundred years earlier? Was the man a friend or foe?

"Scallywag," the man scoffed and raised his shoulders as if he was ready to duel.

The enemy was in front of Lafitte! The insult stung and only someone from the early 1800s would know that term. Lafitte was thankful his pistol in his sash was constantly loaded. The one and only time his gun was empty left him with a bullet hole in his left arm, a gift from an adversary. He wouldn't make that mistake again.

As the leader of the pack plucked at his garb, Lafitte pulled out of his hard gaze with the foe. "Hey man, great costume." The young man, nor any of his cohorts, didn't seem to notice the addition to their entourage.

The five men laughed and one knocked shoulders with him. "Oh, sorry, man." He also admired Lafitte's attire. "Great costume. Wanna join us at Coop's Place?" The man nodded toward the bar up Decatur Street.

"Is that Son of a Biscuit Eater invited?" Lafitte snarled about the enemy.

"Huh? What? No, man, the five of us are good."

"Five? I see six of you." When Lafitte looked again, the man who cast the insult was gone.

Lafitte cursed under his breath and drowned in thought. Who was that man and where did he go? It was as if he disappeared into the night. Was he seeing things? Did too many nights on *The Pride* affect his sight? Or did he have a new ability to now see things that a normal man couldn't? Was the man a ghost? Losing their patience with him, the jovial group of men gave up on their invitation and went on their way.

Without checking for oncoming traffic, Lafitte took a few steps onto Decatur. In an instant, a car to Lafitte's right screeched to a halt inches from him and blared its horn. He had seen vehicles from *The Pride* but this was the first time he came face to face with one. The driver shook his fist and yelled, "Hey dumbass! You gotta watch for cars!"

Lafitte pressed his lips together in annoyance and didn't break stride. As the car drove off, St. Philip Street stretched in the foggy darkness in front of him. He remembered it was the straightest path to his destination. Twenty people gathered around a woman dressed in a vampire outfit as she regaled haunted tales and local legends of the city. Orange, green, and yellow Greek revival-style buildings lit up in the night around them. On Lafitte's right, impaired clientele wandered in and out of MRB Bar. More gawked at him from the second-story wrought-iron balcony.

"You heading to a Halloween party, Jack Sparrow?" a woman wearing a witch costume shouted from above. "Can we come?" She cackled and jabbed her nearby friends in the arm with her elbow.

Lafitte glanced up at her and smiled wide. He didn't know who Jack Sparrow was but the wench was beautiful. Two hundred years had passed since he bedded a woman. He needed skin-on-skin contact. Along with drinking and gambling, the fairer sex was his vice. They had been readily available to him at any brothel with their open bosomed blouses and tight corsets where he could crack Jenny's teacup. He missed their company.

"Aye, belle gosse." Spreading his arms out and maintaining eye contact, he bowed deeply from the sidewalk below her. The idea of a Halloween party eluded him, but he wanted her by his side.

Just then, her friend said, "We gotta go," and yanked the beautiful harlot inside away from Lafitte's sight.

His lust shattered instantly, but he would not be deterred. Grazing the brim of his hat, he saluted the space from where she stood. From the river, he had seen many wenches wandering the streets of the French Quarter. He could have his pick. But first, he had a curse to break.

With a determined gait, he headed a few more blocks to his port of call.

Chapter 2

On the northeast side of the French Quarter, a group of guys invaded Lafitte's Blacksmith Shop Bar and wandered through the mid-October crowd. The inside and out were full as standing-room-only customers filled in empty spaces. Many of them wore Halloween costumes.

"Jules! Can you get those customers for me? We're three-deep tonight." Leah Broussard shouted to her friend from the bar. "It's nuts in here!" Leah filled cup after cup of draft beer and set them on a tray. She was a favorite amongst the male patrons with her tall and lean body. She constantly had glitter in her hair from all of the local festivals and parades. With her exotic looks and natural springy curls, Leah needed little makeup. Her direct Black Creole ancestry ran deep in the city.

"On it." Juliet Vance quickly tossed the remnants of used glasses into a sink and rushed over to the group of guys waiting to place their order. She leaned across the counter to hear them in the noisy bar. Rock music blared from overhead speakers as French Quarter locals and tourists settled in for the night. "What can I get you?" she hollered to the guys.

The one dressed in a cowboy outfit spoke, "Three voodoo daiquiris." He nodded toward the slushie mixer behind Juliet that churned out what the locals called Purple Drank. Two cups of the violet-hued cocktail could sedate a mule that pulled carriages in nearby Jackson Square.

"Coming up." Juliet filled three cups full of the frozen daiquiri and exchanged them with the guy for $30 in cash.

"Keep the change." He grinned at her.

"Thanks."

"When you get off, you wanna save a horse and ride a cowboy?" He winked at her and tipped his fake hat.

Normally, Juliet would have a snappy comeback, but her ego had recently been bruised. And her confidence took a hit. "Umm." She stared at him blankly and dropped her mouth into an O. She couldn't even muster an annoyed groan or an eye roll. Unamused, the guy led his laughing buddies to another side of the packed bar.

Three weeks earlier, Juliet heard the two words that made most people want to crawl into a hole: "You're fired." The sting still hurt. She had worked at Willa Jean in the Central Business District for two years and loved her job. Even though it wasn't Carnival season, loyal customers flocked to the bakery. Learning from the best, Juliet had hoped to eventually take the helm at her own boulangerie. Those dreams shattered like the scorched crust of a crème brûlée when *The Times-Picayune* food critic choked on a plastic baby doll. The hidden trinket in Juliet's off-season king cake sent him to the ER. He surely wouldn't be hosting the next king cake party. Her James Beard-award-winning boss couldn't risk bad press and fired Juliet on the spot. Other bakeries in the city heard what happened and she was immediately black-balled in The Big Easy bakery circuit. The purple, gold, and green dessert was now her kryptonite.

Humiliated, she felt like a failure. After wallowing on her couch for a few days, Juliet found a job tending bar at Lafitte's Blacksmith Shop Bar. The lively tourist spot helped pay the bills until she could find a bakery gig again. The oldest bar in New Orleans had swashbuckling origins. In the late 1700s, Captain Jean Lafitte and his brother Pierre used the building on the corner of Bourbon and St. Philip as a front for their pirate smuggling operations. They stole gold, silver, soap, cloth, dyes, spices, and cocoa from legitimate merchants and then sold the goods at higher prices to private buyers. To misdirect authorities, Pierre was a blacksmith and sold candlesticks, swords, nails, bolts, and axes out of the shop. Little electricity lit the building. Candlelight bounced off sequined Halloween costumes spreading prismed dots all over the bar.

Juliet pushed an errant piece of long blonde hair behind her ear. She recently added a purple streak running the length of her neck. It matched her artsy chef mentality when she worked at Willa Jean. Now the color rivaled the popular cocktail she served every night. Hoping to lift her spirits, she wore her favorite Blink-182 vintage T-shirt. She was turning 32 soon, just in time for the holidays.

She took the order of a new customer dressed in a devil costume.

"Hey, Leah." As she shouted across the noisy tavern, Juliet flipped the Abita handle on the tap system and filled a pint of the local lager. "When do you get off tonight?" Simultaneously, she handed the devil-dressed patron his beer and caught the attention of the next person in line. Four shelves of liquor lined the brick wall behind her. Amber-colored Jim Beam, Bacardi, Jameson, and Kahlua bottles decorated the aged but genteel historic bar.

"Midnight. You?" Leah handed out drinks to other customers at the other end of the bar.

"I'm closing. Derek'll be here later to help me."

An hour later, Juliet made her way through the full dining area. A clown, a fairy princess, and a customer dressed in a British beef eater's outfit clustered around the wooden tables. The only light in that part of the bar came from jar candles. The owner of the bar had kept the establishment as closely aligned to its origins, only allowing candlelight as was the case in the 1700s. In keeping with the tradition, a weathered-stone fireplace in the middle of the room gave off heat in the winter.

The structure of the building featured the Briquette-Entre-Poteaux style used in French Louisiana and withstood two great city fires at the turn of the 19th Century. Two major rooms served patrons: the bar area and the sitting room in the back of the building. Nowadays, it was a popular spot to get a relaxing drink at the far end of raucous Bourbon Street. Tonight, the piano sat silent since their regular musician had called off sick.

A group of guys around Juliet's age called her over to their table with a finger wave. They wore an assortment of football jerseys and passed them off as Halloween costumes.

"What can I get you guys?" Juliet leaned on the table in front of them.

"A round of fireballs," the one wearing an Atlanta Falcons jersey answered.

"Coming up." Juliet nodded toward the football team's name on his chest. "You think that's a good idea wearing that in here?"

"I'll take my chances," he said. "Maybe if you'll take your chances on me?"

"Not in that shirt," she smirked. "I'll be right back with your drinks."

When she returned, Juliet passed shots of the cinnamon whiskey around the table. "You starting a tab?"

"Yeah." The guy in the Falcons jersey handed her his credit card as she ran it through her handheld sales machine. Then he nodded toward a vintage picture on the wall behind Juliet. "Is that Lafitte?"

She turned and locked her eyes on the etched, faded drawing of Jean Lafitte the Pirate. The privateer crossed his arms and held a commanding look in his fierce eyes. The picture gave her the creeps, but she couldn't let her customers know and risk not getting a nice tip.

"Yeah, that's him." Juliet faced the men again. "My coworker told me that picture's cursed."

"No way," the guys said in unison.

Juliet shrugged. "That's what she said. Told me anyone who has possession of it outside of the tavern will have bad luck."

"No way," they said again.

"She said some guy stole it a few years ago and then brought it back to us because of all of the bad luck he had. We've left it on that wall ever since."

"Whoa."

The one wearing the Falcons jersey spoke again, "I heard this place is haunted. And that there are devil eyes in the corner. You ever see anything weird like that going on?"

"I've only been here a couple of weeks, so no." Juliet jerked her head toward the bar. "Go talk to Leah if you want to hear some more stories. She's been here a while and she'll keep you entertained." Juliet glanced at the guys' still-full shots. "Can I get you anything else?"

The guys shook their heads and Juliet walked off to check on other customers.

Right after midnight, Leah found Juliet at the end of the bar. "Hey Jules, I'm heading out. I opened today and I'm beat. Be careful tonight." The crowd around them seemed to shrink in half from the previous hour.

"I always am. Derek'll be here soon. He texted me he's on his way."

"Okay. See you Monday."

Juliet hugged her new friend and Leah's head of brown curls bounced against Juliet's face. Remnants of glitter sprinkled on the floor. They both had the next day off and Juliet was thankful for the break. She had worked six days in a row and she wanted to relax on her couch with a good trashy book.

Fifteen minutes after Leah left, Derek pushed through the door. A former bouncer at a nightclub on the other end of Bourbon Street, he now managed the tavern and helped close up at night. The schedule was perfect for the now-family man. He could spend the afternoon with his kids and work at night after they went to bed.

"Sorry I'm late," he said to Juliet as he dropped his keys on the counter. "Aneeka's sick and the twins wouldn't go to sleep for me. Guess they only want their mama." He sighed in defeat. For as big of a man as he was, his two-year-old twins bested him. He rubbed a hand over his bald head. "I used to have hair before the kids were born."

Juliet laughed. "It's okay. Nothing happened since Leah went home. A couple of guys hit on me, but that was it." She waved a hand toward the hum of the bar where the customers mingled.

"That's an occupational hazard of being a woman in this place."

"Like the girls who used to work here two hundred years ago and got groped all the time. They should have complained more."

In an instant, a giant bottle of Jim Beam fell from a top shelf, nearly missing Juliet, and shattered on the floor. The noise of the tavern immediately came to a halt.

"What the--?" Juliet jumped. "That thing almost knocked me out."

"He's angry again." Derek grabbed a nearby broom to clean up the glass.

"Who's angry?"

"Jean Lafitte."

"Seriously? You believe in that stuff?" Bending down to help, Juliet cocked her head to the side and glared at him, unconvinced. "You sure it's not the crooked old building? Maybe the shelves have shifted?"

"Jules, this whole city's full of ghosts. It was built on pirates, cheats, and prostitutes. Beggars, orphans, and the wrongly accused were brought here from France. They were exiled here in chains, taken of their own free will, and branded with a fleur-de-lis on their shoulders to mark them as under sentence for life. They formed this city on anger and they haven't left. Try to find me a building that's *not* haunted."

Derek carefully put the glass shards into the trash. "It's not only Jean Lafitte at this place. I've been here and candles will go out without explanation. The piano will play on its own. Some people claim they've seen Lafitte standin' by the fireplace. And though I've never seen them myself, there are phantom red eyes that hang around the back dark corner. People have told me there's never a body, never a voice.... only piercin' red eyes. As soon as they make eye contact with it, the eyes freeze, before fadin' into nothin'."

"For real?" Juliet raised an eyebrow and held a dustpan for Derek.

"Yep. There's a female ghost upstairs too. One time, I was here openin' up with Leah. She was downstairs at the bar and I was outside sweepin'. When I came inside, she told me she thought I was upstairs because she heard footsteps on the second floor and someone talkin' to themselves. We went upstairs and no one was there. It was creepy. That's why no one's allowed to close up by themselves."

"Then I'm glad you're here."

Derek put the last of the broken glass in the trash. "You'd think if the ghosts can make a mess like this, why can't they move a broom and clean up after themselves?" Derek rubbed his bald head. "The ghosts don't seem to mind that we're here, so we try to coexist."

"Maybe the ghosts are your typical New Orleans drinkers reluctant to leave their favorite bar?" Juliet laughed.

Chapter 3

At 3:00 a.m., after the last customer left, Derek and Juliet canvassed the tavern and locked up the windows. Even though Juliet had closed up before, the bottle flying off the shelf earlier freaked her out. As they picked up discarded glasses, lifted chairs upside down onto tables, and swept the room, Juliet thought back to other unexplainable things that had happened in the short time she had worked there. A door had mysteriously closed on its own. Candles had died out. The piano played a few notes on its own. Was it the wind? Or had something supernatural done it? Were the ghosts real?

Juliet wiped down a sticky table in the back sitting room. Surprised, she caught a glimpse of a late-comer near the front bar. He looked out of place in a long red velvet coat, but maybe he was dressed up for a Halloween party.

Derek followed her gaze. "Jules, can you take care of that guy?"

"Sure thing." Juliet left Derek and crossed into the front room. "Sorry, buddy, we're closed." She approached the peculiar stranger from the side and pointed toward the door. Maybe he would take the hint and leave without issue.

"Belle gosse, I am Captain Jean Lafitte here on the two-hundredth new moon of October to claim what was once mine." Lafitte took a step toward her, stood up straight, and expansively spread his arms. "This is my place."

Facing him, Juliet scoffed and rolled her eyes. "I don't care who you are, but we're closed and you need to leave." She stepped toward the front door and held it open for him.

"I am not leaving until I retrieve my booty." Lafitte stood his ground.

Juliet yelled to the back room. "Hey, Derek! We got another crazy drunk out here."

"I'm comin', Jules," Derek hollered.

"Jewels?" Lafitte shot an interested look toward Juliet.

"Yeah, Jules," she repeated. "My name is Juliet and everyone calls me Jules."

"You are Jewels."

"Yeah, sure, I'm Jules." Juliet blew out an exasperated sigh.

"Then you are The Named One who must help me," Lafitte proclaimed. "You are The Named One I need. You are Jewels."

"What?" Juliet dismissed him with a chuckle. Derek stepped into the bar area beside her and she spoke to him.

"This guy thinks he's Jean Lafitte and that I'm the chosen one."

"Sounds like something Obi-Wan would say." Derek glanced at the stranger. "Sure looks like a real pirate, but I'm sure he's a drunk. I'll take care of it."

Derek approached Lafitte and laid a heavy hand on his shoulder. The former bouncer knew how to diffuse a situation before it escalated. He had spent many nights checking IDs and tossing out unruly drunks. "Why don't you and I take a walk outside?"

Lafitte lowered his chin and glared at Derek, then to Juliet, and back at Derek. "Remove your hand from me, you scoundrel."

Derek blew out an annoyed sigh and locked eyes with Lafitte. "If you don't leave now while I'm askin' you to, you don't want to see me when I'm not so polite. How about I call you a Lyft?"

"You are lifting me?" Lafitte raised an eyebrow toward Derek, then smiled devilishly. "After all, I am the captain."

"Yeah. And I'm the queen of the Nile." Derek pulled his phone out of his pocket and tapped a finger on it. Then he escorted Lafitte to the door where Juliet stood, watching. "Go outside and wait."

Lafitte stepped onto the dark sidewalk and scanned the surroundings. Before he could comment, Juliet locked him out.

"What a whack job." Juliet shook her head. "I know there are some nutty people in this city, but geez."

"Just you wait," Derek laughed. "The week of Halloween, when the moon is full, the crazies will be out in full force! It's not called Halloween around here, but Halloweek. We'll have people thinking they're vampires and voodoo queens."

For the next fifteen minutes, they cleaned the rest of the bar, closed out receipts, and locked the windows. Then Derek walked Juliet home like he had every time they closed together. Since parking in The Quarter was at a premium and the centuries-old narrow streets always seemed to be under construction, almost everyone walked everywhere, regardless of the time of day -- or night.

"Did you really call him a Lyft?" Juliet asked.

"Nah, I was textin' Aneeka seein' how she's feelin'. That guy's on his own."

The moonless night was fresh around them, as a few drunken tourists wandered past them heading northeast on Bourbon Street toward the residential area.

"I love this part of town at night," Juliet mused as they walked past lamp posts casting shadows on two-hundred-year-old candy-colored homes. "It's an eerie, haunted, and beautiful place. Like no other place I've ever lived."

"That's right, you're a Yankee, darlin'," Derek chuckled. "I sometimes forget that you aren't from here."

"Because I don't have a southern accent? And where I'm from, if you call someone darlin', you'll get a funny look. Maybe even a fist up your nose."

"You're taken in by the romanticism of this city. This dirty, decrepit city." Derek sidestepped a broken section of the sidewalk.

"Yes, I am. But you're still here."

"Yeah, well, like you, despite what I just said, I love this city. It seduces you with mystery and ambiance. Every corner tells a story. Every buildin' has a history. The food is unlike anythin' I've ever eaten. The music has soul and a piece of it goes with you. Even though we have to deal with crazy drunks and entitled tourists, I wouldn't want to live anywhere else."

"The city is offbeat, loud, and proud," Juliet said.

"Like gumbo." Derek laughed out loud.

Juliet's mouth watered at the thought. She had tasted tomato-laden gumbo up north, but it paled in comparison to the local recipes full of Cajun sausage and homemade roux, shunning the heathen tomatoes.

She mused, "The air is rich, sweet, rancid, and hauntingly beautiful. I love getting up right after the sun rises and walking around. The streets are empty and I feel like the whole city is mine. I can stop and admire the different homes, take pictures of things I've never seen before, and take in history. It's like I can feel the city breathing around me."

Beside them, larger-than-life skeletons and zombies decorated Creole cottages while a gargantuan papier-mâché spider spun her web across a front stoop. An overabundance of orange and purple lights lit their path along the quieter end of Bourbon Street. The lights were so bright that Juliet could read a cookbook by them. Around them, a smooth aroma of bergamot, Italian mandarin with tuberose, transparent amber, and benzoin filled the air.

They strolled toward Marigny where Juliet lived on Burgundy Street. Because they liked being different, New Orleanians pronounced it "burGUNdy." Accenting the first syllable, like the boring Yankees did, seemed unfathomable in the city that was in a class by itself. Crossing Esplanade Avenue, they stopped on the neutral ground waiting for a truck to pass. The oak trees above them threw eerie shadows on the ground, like demons from the underworld trying to pull them below.

Even the blind could feel the power of the city.

On the next block, where Bourbon turned into Pauger Street, a few cars passed Juliet and Derek casting mystical beams from their headlights onto the nearby homes. While they waited for the cars to pass, Juliet looked behind them and saw a man in a long red coat on the sidewalk a few houses away.

"Doesn't that look like the drunk we kicked out?" She pointed toward the stranger who was walking toward them.

Derek turned and shrugged. "Maybe. Maybe he lives here?"

"I know most of my neighbors, at least by sight, and, until tonight, I've never seen him before." Juliet furrowed her eyebrows as she tried to place the man but came up empty.

"I wouldn't worry about it. If he bothers you, text me and I'll be here in five."

They made their way along Pauger Street, and the stranger's heels clicked in the distance behind them. On the next block, they turned on Burgundy. Juliet lived on the right side of a bright yellow double-shotgun house. The shotgun design featured houses as narrow as twelve feet wide, stretching deep into the backyard. The homes arranged rooms one behind the other with doors at each end of the house. Despite local legend saying someone could fire a shot from the front door to the back door without hitting anything, the design allowed for excellent airflow in the humid Gulf-shore summers before air conditioning became more commonplace.

Derek escorted Juliet to her tiny cement stoop that led to her front door. Creating an Easter egg look, pale blue floor-to-ceiling shutters flanked both sides of the old wooden door. A magnolia tree provided shade in the postage-stamp backyard.

"I love this house." Juliet sighed and smiled as she unlocked the door. Five years earlier, she fell in love with its long and narrow features and bought the house. Even though she was a transplant from Baltimore, the neighbors on her brightly-colored block welcomed her with open arms. Within minutes of meeting them, she learned about their Katrina experience, their family, their pets, reading preferences, and what music they liked. The neighborhood had a hundred stories to tell. Across the street, Juliet could see her neighbor Mr. Landry smoking a cigarette. The small red flame was the only light on his porch. He liked to wait up for her to make sure she got home safe. She smiled knowing he liked to protect her.

Juliet loved that she could walk a block in any direction and find cafés, clubs, and restaurants. When she wanted to venture a little further, she made her way to The Spotted Cat on Frenchmen Street to listen to live music. She had gone there a few times with Derek and Leah on their nights off to listen to the Crawdaddy Jazz Band.

"What're you doin' tomorrow?" Derek asked.

Juliet yawned. "Sleeping in. I don't know how you close all the time."

"This is early for me. When I bounced at Saints and Sinners, we weren't out of there until almost 5:00. Sometimes we'd see the sun come up."

"You don't sleep?"

"When my kids do."

Juliet rolled her eyes at Derek because she knew that amount of sleep wasn't enough. After she got some much-needed shut-eye, she had plans to make a batch of biscuits in the morning and hand them out to her favorite street musicians.

"I'll see you Monday."

"Good night. *Darlin'*." Derek offered a toothy grin.

Juliet laughed. As she stepped into her front room, Derek headed home on the quiet, fall night.

Chapter 4

The next morning, Juliet awoke at 10:30 to the sight of her neighbors walking their dogs and getting their Sunday morning coffee at Horn's Eatery. The half-mile walk was worth sitting among locals and getting the best comfort food in the area. Tourists didn't usually wander this deep into the Marigny unless they had been told about the hidden gem.

The framed quote on Juliet's nightstand reminded her every day why she loved her adopted city. "For what it's worth: it's never too late or, in my case, too early to be whoever you want to be. There's no time limit, stop whenever you want. You can change or stay the same, there are no rules to this thing. We can make the best or the worst of it. I hope you make the best of it. And I hope you see things that startle you. I hope you feel things you never felt before. I hope you meet people with a different point of view. I hope you live a life you're proud of. If you find that you're not, I hope you have the courage to start all over again." Most people learned of the quote from F. Scott Fitzgerald's short story *The Curious Case of Benjamin Button*. Juliet took it to heart.

She threw on some jeans and an old Baltimore Ravens T-shirt that her dad had given her before he passed away. The shirt had lasted through him teaching her how to make Maryland crab cakes and early mornings at her mother's bakery. Juliet would wake up at 5:00 and watch her mother mold cinnamon rolls bigger than her fist. Customers lined the sidewalk for her mom's red velvet cookies. Juliet's mother created special-order cheesecakes with a sweet, tangy, creamy, and rich perfect balance. This was where Juliet's love for baking blossomed.

After her mother died a few years after her father, Juliet moved from the Charm City to the Crescent City. She had bounced around a few small bakeries and then found her way to Willa Jean. *Condé Nast Traveler* reviewed the retro-chic café with "Award-winning biscuits and breakfast served with aplomb." There, Juliet learned to make local favorites like bruto cookies and the famous King Cake full of cinnamon, caramel, and cream cheese. She had found her calling.

Getting fired still hurt. If she was going to find another bakery gig, she needed to make her delicious concoctions regularly to keep her recipes and mind fresh. Slinging drinks at an old tavern could keep her interested for only so long. In her kitchen, Juliet worked at the island in the center of the room. Windows above the sink on one wall faced the original 1850s brick fireplace on the opposite wall. Her tool roll was full of a silicone pastry bag, four tips, a spatula, a whisk, a scraper, a channel knife, and measuring spoons.

Pioneer biscuit mix, sour cream, a bottle of Abita amber beer, and a bag of pork cracklings laid out in front of her. Cracklin' Biscuits were on the menu this morning. She blended everything, dropped small mounds onto a baking sheet, put them in the oven, and set the timer. Juliet was still afraid to make a King Cake, her nemesis. The shock of being fired because of it still haunted her. While the biscuits baked, she whipped up a batch of cane syrup butter. They wouldn't be authentic without Steen's cane syrup.

As Juliet creamed the ingredients, a clattering sound on her back patio interrupted her.

"What the--"

She peeked through the back door window and jumped back. The stranger dressed as a pirate who she had kicked out of the bar sat on her metal patio furniture twirling his mustache between his fingers.

Frantic, Juliet yanked her phone out of her purse, finding the battery dead. In her tired state the night before, she forgot to plug it in before she went to bed. She thought of running to Derek's house a few blocks away, but would that do her any good? And would the man follow her?

She cautiously spied on the costumed man through her window, hoping he'd leave on his own. He didn't get up.

Instead, he twirled his mustache with a slight uptick in his mouth as if he pondered something interesting. His calmness took the forefront. He didn't *seem* like he was there to hurt her. She figured he would have forced his way inside if that was the case.

Juliet slowly opened her door. The creaking sound alerted him and he turned in her direction.

"Jewels." The stranger stood and bowed to Juliet. His long red cloak fell past his knees and gave way to a gold-handled sword on his hip.

"How... how do you know my name?" She didn't take her eyes off the weapon but he did not attempt to reach for it.

"Last night, your gentleman friend called you Jewels at my tavern."

"Yeah, he called me Jules. So?"

"Jewels."

"Right. Jules." Juliet was getting more and more annoyed with the name tête-à-tête. The joke was getting old quickly.

"You are The Named One I need," the man proclaimed. "You are Jewels."

"The named one you need for what?"

"Let me introduce myself." The stranger stood tall and puffed out his chest. "I am Captain Jean Lafitte the Pirate."

Juliet laughed heartily, wiping an errant tear of joy from her eye. "Oh, come on." She leaned against her open door, ready to slam it shut if anything peculiar happened.

"'Tis true. I am him. And you are The Named One to help me find my treasure. I have less than a fortnight to find and return them."

"You have the wrong person," Juliet spoke through a chuckle. "I don't know anything about a treasure." She wished her cell phone was charged so that she could call Derek with this hilarious story.

"You must help me." The man took a step closer to her.

Juliet's humor turned to alarm. She stared at the sword at his sash and gulped. Her skin flushed.

"I am not here to hurt you."

"Then... then... what're you here for?" Juliet stammered, her voice increasing in pitch and volume. She glanced around her small yard to see if he had any accomplices. She didn't see any. If she wanted to flee, the only way to get her freedom was back through her house. Hopefully, he didn't force his way in. Her chest tingled and her heart raced.

"I told you. You will help me find my treasure." He smiled widely at her.

"I'm sorry. I can't help you." Juliet dashed back inside and locked the door. Immediately, she plugged in her phone. As she waited for her biscuits to finish baking, she watched Jean Lafitte through her window again. He did not attempt to leave. Nor come into her house. She couldn't will her phone to charge fast enough. Maybe she was imagining things? Was he fallout from her working so late the previous night? She was already not her normal self after getting fired and this added to it. Maybe she needed some fresh air to clear her head.

After her biscuits were done, Juliet shoved them in individual baggies and then into a poly bag that she slung on her shoulder. By then, her phone had charged 25%.

"Good enough." She pushed her phone into her back pocket and quietly left through her front door. She couldn't risk the delusional pirate hearing her leave. He had to have still been drunk from the night before. There was no other explanation. She was thankful he didn't try to attack her. She was lucky. The situation could have been a lot worse and she would have been on the front page of *The Times-Picayune*. The headline would read: "Pirate makes mincemeat out of pastry chef."

As Juliet stepped off of her porch, she waved to her next-door neighbor. "Mornin', Mrs. Hebert."

"Mornin', Juliet." The older woman waved back as she simultaneously stroked the Shih Tzu resting in her lap. Mrs. Hebert had lived in the Marigny most of her life, raising six children. She lived alone now, except for her pooch Scarlett.

Juliet made her way along Burgundy Street toward Esplanade, her fear and anxiety decreasing as she passed each sherbet-colored house. An iron gate attached to a home creaked open by itself. Juliet didn't think anything of it. Maybe the gate was on crooked ground. After all, this was New

Orleans. The city was full of uneven sidewalks and disfigured fences, all victims of the ever-changing life below sea level.

Mornings like this were quiet. Juliet loved to walk through her neighborhood as the sun rose above the mighty Mississippi. She loved the scent of southern magnolia, fresh jasmine, and a kiss of musk in the air. A few dogs barked and a handful of shop owners unlocked their doors before the tourists took over the cool morning. Living in New Orleans was unlike anything else. People in the city were under a spell of something greater than them. Was it the signs of past residents who refused to leave?

At the corner of Burgundy and Esplanade, a trumpeter tooted some ragtime tunes outside of Buffa's Bar. A poster for Orphaned in Storyville touted the band's next gig. The old neighborhood live music hall had been around since 1939. Juliet wondered if Louis Armstrong had ever played there. She imagined him singing "La Vie En Rose;" his raspy voice floating into the night.

The musician lowered his brass horn. "Hey Juliet, where y'at?"

"All right, where y'at, Nate?" Juliet reached into her bag and handed the older man a biscuit. "Here ya go." She first met Nate a year earlier when she strolled through her neighborhood. She had walked by him many times before and finally stopped to tell him she enjoyed his music. Ever since, she'd bring him one of her goodies and he'd play her one of his soulful melodies.

"Thank you, sha." His weary eyes twinkled and the wrinkles in his forehead seemed to form a smile. He wore a silver button-down shirt, the sheen glistened in the morning sun.

Across the street, at the Melrose Mansion hotel, one of the long black window shutters slammed shut. The unexpected noise made Juliet and Nate stop talking and glance up.

"That was weird," she said. "That happen before?"

Nate shook his head. "Not that I heard."

"Ah, well, I'll see you in a few days. I'll have more goodies for you then."

"*Laissez les bon temps rouler.*" He tipped his trumpet in salute toward Juliet and she was on her way.

Living so close to death in New Orleans with the threat of hurricanes, floods, and, historically, yellow fever, locals had to have a positive attitude. Life was too short for them. New Orleans was a city with many faces, but only one soul. Its mystery and ambiance could seduce anyone. Once in its clutches, it will never let go.

Juliet made a right in front of Buffa's and stopped on the neutral ground on Esplanade. A young man strummed a guitar under one of the massive oak trees as if it was his oldest friend. Juliet stopped, said hello, and handed him a biscuit.

She crossed the grassy strip. When she reached the sidewalk, a rocking chair on a nearby porch of an old mansion rocked slowly back and forth. Juliet thought maybe someone recently got up and went inside. The porch was decorated with small pumpkins and gourds. She noticed that her shoe was untied and knelt to tie it.

"Jewels," a man's voice came from behind her. "I have found you again."

Juliet looked up to see Jean Lafitte still dressed in his red cloak and his sword against his hip. She rolled her eyes and shook her head in annoyance. How many times did she have to tell him she wasn't interested in helping him? She stood up to face him.

"Look–" she started to say, but before she could utter another word, Lafitte jerked his head toward the moving rocking chair.

"That is enough!" He yelled to the empty rocker.

Clearly, the man was crazy and belonged in a mental hospital, Juliet thought. Now he was talking to empty rocking chairs.

"I won't tolerate that kind of talk about you."

"What kind of talk? I don't hear anything."

"You didn't hear that man comment on your voluptuous curves as you bent over? He is no gentleman."

"No... What man?" Juliet raised her eyebrows in confusion.

"You do not see him?"

"No."

"He's right there--" Lafitte pointed to the empty porch. "Surely, you must. You cannot see him, but I can."

"Sorry." Juliet shrugged. She should have been freaked out, but oddly she wasn't.

"Hmmm." Lafitte furrowed his eyebrows and then bowed toward Juliet. "I must apologize. He does not understand that I request your assistance and that you would be offended by his words."

"I don't see or hear anyone." Juliet looked back at the empty porch.

"You still do not see the old Frenchman in the white ruffled shirt and riding boots sitting in the chair?" Lafitte gestured to the rocker. "His foul language is not welcome."

"Nooo...." Juliet was unconvinced. The only thing she was convinced of was that the man in front of her was delusional.

"I said that is enough, you codfish!" Lafitte yelled back at the porch. By now the rocking chair had stopped moving.

In an instant, one of the small pumpkins on the porch flew through the air toward Jean Lafitte as if someone had thrown it. Lafitte saw it coming, jumped out of the way, and the pumpkin smashed on the sidewalk beside Juliet.

Her mouth fell into an O.

"I– You– What–" Words escaped her as she realized what had happened in front of her. She was barely able to move. She stared at him with wide eyes. "You are..." She pointed at Jean Lafitte with a wobbly finger.

"Captain Jean Lafitte the Pirate." He smiled broadly and bowed deeply toward her again.

"But that–" Juliet still could not find her words. She stared at the empty porch, wondering if the Frenchman was still there. Her legs wobbled, and she needed to sit down.

"That," Lafitte explained, "was a resident who has never left this city. Like I have never left." He motioned toward Burgundy Avenue. "And like the other residents on your walk who opened the iron gate and slammed the wooden shutter."

Juliet gasped and, in shock, dropped her bag full of biscuits on the cement. "How– How did you know?"

"Apparently, I can see and hear them and you cannot. I discovered it last night on the way to my tavern. At the tavern where I met you. And you will help me find my treasure. Because you are Jewels."

"Look, maybe you can see these ghosts and all, and that's cool, but I can't help you find the jewels."

"You helped those musicians with your food. Why will you not help me? I have less than a fortnight to find and return them. Before the moon is full. Time is running out."

Juliet raised a hand to her forehead and shook her head in frustration. "Fine. You win. I get it. You're Jean Lafitte." She still didn't understand everything that he told her, but figured if she didn't accept him for who he was, then he would bug her for the next two weeks until she did. "But why should I believe you're telling the truth? Pirates lie, cheat, and steal to get what they want. They even murder and rape." She picked up her bag of biscuits and slung it back on her shoulder.

"Aye, belle gosse, 'tis true," Lafitte snorted with a bemused grin. "I have stolen many a treasure in my prime. But the last treasure I pilfered cursed me and my crew 200 years ago and we have lived in purgatory on the mighty river ever since. That is why I am here now. To break the curse."

Even though she still didn't trust him, Juliet's interest was piqued. When she moved to New Orleans, she had heard stories of local legends where ghosts haunted every other building. One tale described a ghost ship watching from the Mississippi. Many drunks at the tavern claimed to have seen it bobbing along the edge of the river. She had brushed off their inebriated nonsense. Until now.

"Hmmm." Juliet's forehead wrinkled and she squinted at Lafitte.

"You are still unconvinced."

As he reached for his gold-handled cutlass, Juliet quickly leaned away, color rising in her cheeks. She considered whacking him with her bag of biscuits and running off. But he found her when she left her house so she was certain he would find her again.

Lafitte spoke again as he raised his sword upright in front of her, not at her. "I swear to you on the soul of my brother

Pierre that I am telling the truth. He gave me this sword before he died from fever in Mexico. He was the last man I ever trusted."

"Okay." Juliet nodded slowly. She had seen *The Princess Bride* enough times to know that when pirates swear on the soul of a loved one, it's legitimate. "I'll help you."

"Very well." Lafitte lowered his sword and puffed out his chest. His enigmatic smile stretched under his mustache.

"But first let me deliver the rest of these biscuits. You can come with me, but don't do anything stupid. But then again, this city's full of freaks. You'll blend right in if you talk to another ghost. It's the normal ones who stand out." Juliet shook her head and rolled her eyes. Each moment added one more notch to the already bizarre situation. She couldn't believe she agreed to help a pirate find a treasure in the middle of Halloween season.

Only in New Orleans.

Chapter 5

After Juliet delivered the rest of her biscuits, she and Jean Lafitte made their way to Café Du Monde. The open-air coffee shop on Decatur was packed with tourists and locals chowing down on beignets and sipping café au lait. Powdered sugar from the beignets left a sticky sheen all over the floor, chairs, and tables. An earthy aroma of chicory filled the air. Music serenaded them.

"Come on. I'll buy you a snack." Juliet led Lafitte to the line of people waiting to be seated.

A young man in the line behind them nodded towards Lafitte's tricorn hat and said, "Hey Jack Sparrow, nice outfit. I saw the rest of your crew around."

"My name is not Jack Sparrow." Lafitte straightened his shoulders and pointed to himself. "I am Jean Lafitte."

"Whatever, man." The youngster turned away and scrolled through his phone.

"Who is this Jack Sparrow?" Lafitte asked Juliet, with a furrowed brow. "That is the second time someone has called me by that name."

She laughed loudly, realizing he didn't know the modern reference. "He's a pirate."

"No..." Lafitte fiercely shook his head. "I have studied every buccaneer in the Gulf. I know my foes. I have never heard of Jack Sparrow. He has no letter of marque."

Juliet chuckled again and pulled her phone out of her pocket. Her thumbs flew over the small screen a few times as Lafitte curiously examined her actions. "Here." She presented an image of Johnny Depp dressed as Jack Sparrow.

Lafitte tilted his head and squinted at the small screen. "I am unfamiliar with him."

"That's because he's fiction," Juliet explained. "He's--"

Before she could explain a movie, Lafitte interrupted her. "And what is this tiny box you and others like that young gentleman carry? I have seen it from a distance from my ship, but do not understand its purpose." The colorful squares and rectangles puzzled him.

"It's a phone. To send texts. Make phone calls." She found Lafitte staring blankly at her with his dark eyes. "We communicate with it."

He snorted. "I communicate by writing letters or sailing my ship to speak to someone in person."

"You don't need to do that anymore. These phones send an immediate message." Before she could dial a number or send a text, a server told them a table had opened up.

A minute later, they sat at the round, metal tables that had overlooked Jackson Square since 1862. Juliet placed an order for the delectable French-style donuts and two cups of café au lait.

"Tell me about this curse." Juliet leaned toward Lafitte who sat across from her. His tall and slender frame relaxed into the metal chair. "But wait, wait--" Juliet threw up a dismissive hand, quickly glanced to her left and then to her right, and leaned closer. "Are there any ghosts here like that guy on the porch?"

Lafitte perused their surroundings. Servers in white button shirts, black bow ties, and paper hats skirted around the small tables delivering beignets and coffee. Juliet felt the calming air currents as ceiling fans twirled non-stop above her. She tuned out the constant din of the other patrons' chatter to focus on her newfound guest. Lafitte narrowed his eyes, unblinking, as he zeroed in on the top of the giant flood wall that ran between the café and the river.

"What is it?" Juliet looked where he faced.

"An apparition."

"Another ghost?"

"Aye."

"But I don't see anything." Juliet jockeyed to get a better view, but saw nothing except the palm trees and murals that decorated the wall. When the ghostly Frenchman threw a pumpkin at them hours earlier, her belief in the supernatural was piqued even though she didn't see anything now. She wasn't sure what to believe.

"He is dressed in royal garb, with a long coat and hat like mine." Lafitte pointed. "You do not see him?"

"No, I only see the wall." A few café patrons wandered in front of her. "Anyway..." Juliet set her attention on Lafitte. "What's this curse about?"

"Two hundred years ago..." He twirled his handlebar mustache between his fingers. "On one of my voyages, my crew and I sailed *The Pride* through the Caribbean toward the Yucatan and Isla Mujeres--"

"The Island of Women," Juliet interrupted.

"Aye. The island of *beautiful* women," Lafitte mused and gazed off. "We docked there and took advantage of the island's hospitality. After several days of enjoying the curves of the local maidens, imbibing on grog, and eating poc chuc, salbutes, and panuchos, our needs were satiated and we set sail to pursue our next plunder. Before we left the island, we were warned that nothing was to be taken from the island. If we did, we would be cursed. A true buccaneer does not tempt the likes of a curse..."

A server came by and set their beignets and coffee in front of them.

"Do you know what these are?"

"Aye, they were made in France where I lived before I came here."

Juliet took a bite of her powdered sugar treat, never taking her eyes off Jean Lafitte. His story intrigued her.

"As we sailed into the Gulf toward Louisiana, peculiar things happened. Food spoiled after one day. Fresh water was suddenly salty. Our golden loot turned to useless lead overnight. My men came down with unexpected pains in their arms, unable to steer the ship. It took us a fortnight to get to New Orleans when it should have taken three passes of the moon. Our trip to New Orleans would be brief as my brother Pierre was dead and we had no place to set up business. The terrible things continued to happen. We were at a loss until Cedric the Gunner was caught with jewels in his satchel. Jewels from Isla Mujeres. Two rubies, two sapphires, and two emeralds. T'was too late to turn around. Once we docked at the Port of New Orleans, we hanged Cedric until he was dead. He danced with Jack Ketch. His code of conduct was unforgivable by putting the rest of my men at risk. I show no mercy for men like that."

Juliet gasped at the mutinous man's fate.

As Lafitte took a bite of his beignet, he splattered a cloud of powdered sugar all over his red cloak. He cursed under his breath and Juliet laughed. Most newcomers to Café Du Monde made the mistake of wearing dark clothes.

Lafitte continued, "I reconnected with prior unsavory associates in New Orleans and inquired how to lift the curse. A wench at a brothel I had frequented instructed me to find a young belle gosse by the name of Marie Laveau."

"No way!" Juliet slapped the table and nearly spilled her coffee.

"You have heard of her?" Lafitte arched an eyebrow.

"Everyone in New Orleans knows about Marie Laveau. She was the Voodoo Queen of New Orleans. People still put gris-gris on her tomb in St. Louis Cemetery Number One for good luck."

"Interesting." Lafitte tilted his head and pressed his lips together. "I was told she was a young widow looking for work and that she had special powers. The curse needed to be lifted. Otherwise, my whole crew might have found their way to Davy Jones's Locker."

"That's not good." Juliet shook her head.

"Marie came to the ship and inspected the six jewels. She chanted in Haitian words I did not know and banged a small drum. As she did this, she wrote script in a notebook."

"You sat and watched her do this?"

"Aye. T'was our last option. Marie explained that the jewels cursed any man who removed them from Isla Mujeres and gave extraordinary power to women who possessed them."

"You already knew this," Juliet pointed out.

"Aye." Lafitte nodded. "Marie also stated that the jewels could not be separated, or terrible hurricanes would come. An act of God, she said. The only thing I fear is an act of God. I trusted her."

A shiver ran through Juliet as she thought about Hurricanes Katrina and Ida and the devastation they left in their wake.

Lafitte continued, "But then, when it seemed like she came to a conclusion, she proclaimed that she needed to leave the ship immediately otherwise we all risked a terrible demise. I escorted her to the dinghy and pushed her toward the shore."

"That seems normal to me. I mean as normal as it could be." Juliet choked back a laugh.

Lafitte ignored her last comment and continued his tale. "As Marie rode the current and out of reach, she stood, put a hand into the pocket of her flowing robes, and then pulled it back out. She smiled like the devil and opened her fist."

"The jewels were in her hand?" Juliet wanted to know.

"Aye." Lafitte nodded with purpose.

"This is how she became the most powerful voodoo queen in all of New Orleans," Juliet pondered.

"She double-crossed me. No one double-crosses Captain Jean Lafitte and gets away with it. Marie then shouted to us that we were banished to *The Pride* forever. Besides my brother Pierre, she was the last person I trusted."

"Did you go after her?" Juliet sat up straight.

"Before I could, my first-mate Poopdeck Pete jumped in the river after her. Clearly, he knew where his loyalties were. However, it was short-lived. As soon as he hit the rough waters, he was swallowed up whole by a maelstrom. This kind of whirlpool is unheard of on a river. I had only heard tales of one of these in the Atlantic. Never in calm waters."

Juliet's eyes grew wide at his tale.

"Other men in my crew attempted to get in the water and found a similar fate. One shimmied down the side of the ship and lost his leg once it made contact with the water. He now has a peg leg. Another reached in to pull the first one upward and accidentally dropped his hand in the water. He now has a hook where his hand once was. We realized we could never leave the ship again."

Juliet's mouth fell into an O at the repercussions of the curse.

Lafitte went on, "In Marie's haste to leave *The Pride*, she left behind her notebook. T'was her downfall. She indicated that after 200 years she wrote only the captain could leave the ship. I am Captain Jean Lafitte. Only I could leave."

"What if you died and were no longer the captain?"

Lafitte chuckled, "Every self-respecting pirate knows the next in command becomes the captain."

"And your crew is still on board?"

"I gave them orders to stay. No one defies their captain."

Juliet didn't fully understand the chain of command, but nodded nonetheless.

He continued, "Now I must find The Named One to help reverse the hex. You are The Named One. You are Jewels."

"Yeah, my friends call me Jules." Juliet was still unsure how she could help. "But that's a stretch."

Lafitte ignored her again and spoke, "I wasn't sure who Marie meant until I saw you at my tavern. You are The Named One. Marie Laveau also wrote that jewels empower women and that the curse could be lifted starting with the two-hundredth new moon of October."

Remembering seeing something on the wall calendar at the tavern, Juliet said, "That was yesterday."

Lafitte nodded. "Aye. Marie's notes also revealed that I had a fortnight to return the jewels and complete the quest."

"That's two weeks," Juliet replied.

"Aye, before the next full moon disappears, I must find the jewels. If I do not succeed, my crew and I shall be cursed to the river for eternity. That cannot happen. We have waited long enough. I must retrieve the jewels and return them to Isla Mujeres."

Juliet let this news digest as she ate the last of her beignet. Scenarios bounced through her head. What would have happened if she wasn't working last night? Would he still find her and insist that she help him? Would anything happen to her if she didn't help him?

"I have so many questions." Juliet narrowed her eyes and crossed her arms over her chest.

Lafitte raised his open palm in a 'go-on' gesture.

"How have you and your crew survived all of this time?"

"The curse has allowed us to live in purgatory. We do not age. We have drunk the same grog and eaten the same salted beef for two centuries. Our bodies crave something else. Being stationed in one spot is not the life of a privateer. We have held the same crew for the same amount of time. We desire the company of women..." Lafitte leaned closer to Juliet, his eyes burning into her.

Juliet jerked back. "Oh, hell no! Forget it!" It had been a while since she had been with a man, but she wasn't about to give it up for a rakish pirate. She still had some self-respect, even though she had been recently fired.

"Women line the halls of brothels for the intimate company of Jean Lafitte." He smiled coyly at her.

Equally suspicious and intrigued, Juliet sipped on the last of her café au lait. She admired his confidence and brazenness. Juliet knew too many people who followed a pack.

"You are a striking belle gosse," Lafitte purred and reached across the small table and played with the purple streak in Juliet's blonde hair. "But my loins must wait until the jewels are recovered. My ship and my crew must come first."

Juliet choked on her coffee at the double entendre.

Chapter 6

After Juliet paid the bill at Café Du Monde, she led Lafitte south along Decatur, the robust Mississippi on their left.

"You've told me about the curse." Juliet quickly zig-zagged around people on the sidewalk as Jean Lafitte tried to keep up. "But why do you need me?"

Mule-drawn carriages hauling tourists through The Quarter clomped past them. A patient rickshaw driver waited at the corner for customers. Art seekers perused paintings along the iron fence around Jackson Square. The stench of *Decatur-ade* mixed with the hot dog aroma from the Lucky Dog vendor under a red and white umbrella. No one looked twice at Jean Lafitte dressed like a pirate. He was another freak in The Quarter.

"Because you are Jewels," he said with righteous indignation. "You are The Named One. Your name proves that you shall help me. I did not know who The Named One was until I met you."

"I *shall* help you?" Juliet arched an eyebrow. Treasure hunting was not in her wheelhouse. "I admire your optimism, but what makes you think I can and will do it?"

"I know in my gut that you and I shall succeed. I am a successful privateer because I have not failed. When I make a request, it is followed. I am the captain, after all." He tipped his tricorn hat at her.

"But I'm not one of your crew."

"Aye. You are now."

"You said you haven't trusted anyone since your brother. Why do you trust me to help you?"

"I don't."

"You don't?" Juliet stopped walking, stood in place, and eyed him. "What if I take the treasure and run?"

"As I stated before, no one double-crosses me and gets away with it."

"Then why should I help you if you don't trust me?"

"As I promised to all of my crew, the payout is great once the bounty is made."

Unconvinced, Juliet narrowed her eyes. She would need more than a vague answer to join the quest for the jewels.

"No one refuses Jean Lafitte," he boasted.

Juliet laughed out loud. Even though he was serious about his charming effect on women, she couldn't take him seriously. He was two centuries behind in the relationships between men and women. She had a lot to teach him if he was going to survive in modern New Orleans for two weeks. The shameless women who were willing to lift their shirts during Mardi Gras for cheap plastic beads would eat him alive. He might initially enjoy their company but become confused with their modern attitudes if they refused him. With his assuming attitude, he could even get slapped. Even if he didn't trust her, she felt bad for the guy. After the humiliation of getting fired, this adventure could be good for her.

She examined his dated clothing. "Come on. I need to take you somewhere."

On the next block, Juliet led Lafitte into H & M past the Shops at Jax Brewery.

Racks upon racks and tables of clothing greeted them in all colors and sizes. Other patrons scattered around them searching for their own clothes. Intrigued, Lafitte had never bought clothing like this before. He always went to a high-end tailor to make his velvet cloaks and silk tops.

Juliet steered him toward the men's section and held a pair of jeans up to his waist. "What do you think of these?"

Lafitte patted the denim and wrinkled his nose at her. "These are not made of silk. I cannot wear them."

"Well, you can't wear that outfit--" Juliet gestured to his high-end cloak and trousers. "--for the next two weeks. You'll need a change of clothes eventually." Juliet also knew that if he continued to wear his clothes someone would either try to take advantage of him or harass him. He could probably defend himself just fine with his sword and pistol but she didn't want to take the chance. "Try these on to make sure they fit." She also grabbed a blue hoodie from a nearby table.

"Aye." As they stood near the racks of clothes, Lafitte unbuttoned his breeches and dropped them. His attached sword hit the floor with a clank. His flowing shirt barely covered his family jewels.

"Whoa! You can't drop trou in the middle of the store!" Juliet shrieked and averted her eyes.

"You instructed me to try them on."

"Yeah, in the fitting room." Juliet pointed to the sign on the wall behind them. "And don't you wear underwear?"

"I find them too bulky. My linen shirt is never untucked and undergarments add tightness to my trousers." Lafitte proudly stood in front of her, as if he knew what he had to offer.

With her hand covering her eyes, Juliet blindly held the jeans up in front of his half-naked body.

When Jean Lafitte realized he had to yank his leather boots off to try the jeans on, he decided it was too much trouble where he stood. He pulled his breeches back up and smiled broadly at Juliet.

She held the jeans to him and he took them to the dressing room.

A few minutes later, he emerged with a scowl on his face.

"They don't fit?" Juliet asked.

"Aye, but how on earth do I not nick my manhood with that metal jaw on the front? I cannot be maimed for my lovely paramours."

Juliet laughed out loud. "You wear underwear."

Chapter 7

As they left the clothing store with jeans, a hoodie, and a pack of boxers, Jean Lafitte scrutinized the three-story pink building across the street.

"That's Tujague's," Juliet said. "It's the second oldest restaurant in the city."

"No, that is not what I am studying." He examined the midday sky over the cotton candy-colored building. He squinted his eyes and pursed his lips.

"What do you see?" Juliet asked. His unusual power intrigued her.

"Black streaks in the sky."

"Black streaks like what?" To Juliet, the sky was filled with billowing white clouds.

"They are floating above the building, bouncing like ocean waves. Something is there." He stood his ground.

"Well, it *is* New Orleans. That restaurant is known to be haunted. I've heard about doors slamming on their own and china shattering to the floor."

As traffic broke in front of them, Juliet crossed Decatur toward St. Louis Street. "This gives me an idea."

Lafitte rushed to keep up with her. "Where are we headed?"

"You said Marie Laveau double-crossed you," Juliet answered. "Let's go see her."

"She is still alive after all this time?" Lafitte asked.

"Some people in this city think so."

They skirted around tourists meandering along the narrow sidewalk across the street from the Napoleon House. Lafitte stopped and studied the restaurant's sign in the shape of the French emperor's bicorne hat. "That minuscule man still has a congregation here?"

"It's only a restaurant. Don't worry about him." Juliet brushed it off and kept her quick pace, an after-effect from running around a bakery for years. The Quarter was full of historic buildings. "I think back then someone had plotted to rescue Napoleon from his exile and bring him to that building, but it fell through."

"Aye, it was Dominique You, one of my associates." Lafitte hurried behind her. "Nicholas Girod lived in that house." He pronounced the surname as *zhee-ROW*. "He was a wealthy businessman and former mayor and underwrote the failed scheme."

"Good to know." Juliet kept walking along St. Louis Street.

For the next five blocks, they pushed through the heart of the French Quarter. A fresh floral aroma of ylang ylang and lily with notes of vanilla and musk filled their noses. They passed the ostentatious Louisiana Supreme Court House, world-famous Antoine's Restaurant, and the Hermann-Grima House and Museum. Halloween revelers imbibed on drinks on the wrought-iron second-floor galleries above them. Street musicians entertained locals and tourists alike on corner stoops. One tickled the ivories on an upright piano in the middle of the street. Drag queens, genteel Southerners, and mesmerized tourists mingled around them. Everyone was welcome and no one was ostracized. Not one person thought Jean Lafitte was out of place.

When the unlikely duo reached the Jewel of the South restaurant, Rampart Street stretched from side to side in front of them.

"One more block," Juliet instructed Lafitte.

"Where are you taking me?"

"You'll see."

They hurried across Rampart and the neutral ground at Basin Street. As they waited for the streetlight to turn green,

Jean Lafitte spotted a small green signpost. "Lafitte Greenway? 'Tis named after me?"

"Sure. Lots of things are named after you. Funny that we honor our crooks in Louisiana. Hotels, a town, a national park system, restaurants... But that's not why we're here." Juliet pointed to the six-foot white crumbling brick wall in front of them that spanned the entire block. Hurricane Katrina couldn't even knock it down. "That... is why we're here."

"St. Louis Cemetery?"

Juliet smirked when she realized Lafitte had been in New Orleans during the earliest years of the old and hauntingly beautiful cemetery. "Yes. There's a tomb inside I want you to see." She pulled out her phone and quickly ordered two tour tickets online. "We're in. Let's go."

While they waited for the next tour, mourners in black arrived for a funeral first line. Like other things, New Orleans had a unique way to celebrate their dead and put the "fun" in funeral. Once the procession moved from the funeral service to the cemetery, the first line formed of musicians, funeral directors, family, and close friends of the deceased. A brass band was at the ready to bury the dead with music. A somber Christian hymn filled the air. The procession moved toward the family plot. The midday sun reflected off the marble tombs creating an angelic glow. Once the body is laid to rest, the jazz band would pick up the tempo and lead the mourners in jubilation through the streets, adding dancing second-liners along the way. No other U. S. city boasted a tradition like this.

When the next tour started, Juliet and Jean Lafitte entered through the iron gates to the final resting place of the city's most famous and infamous historical figures. The city's oldest extant cemetery spread like a labyrinth in front of them. Crumbling above-ground unique graves hinted at the stories of the larger-than-life personalities entombed within the City of the Dead. Unlike other cemeteries, New Orleans' high water table made in-ground burials impossible. The wall vaults stacked family gravesites one on top of another. High ambient temperatures meant that bodies would decompose quickly. In a year, only the bones would remain. These would then be pushed into a pit at the back of the tomb, creating space for more bodies to be placed in the tomb.

Juliet and Jean Lafitte followed the tour to the left and came upon one of the cemetery's most famous residents. Before them was a tall and narrow delicate tomb surrounded by Halloween trinkets and flowers. Sets of triple Xs covered the tomb scribbled by believers hoping that their wishes would come true.

They stood several feet away from the rest of the tour group while others snapped pictures around them.

"Here she is," Juliet said proudly. "Marie Laveau."

In an instant, Jean Lafitte yanked the gold-handled cutlass from his sash and raised it at the tomb. "You have double-crossed--"

"Whoa!" Juliet interrupted him and slapped a calming hand on his forearm. The clothing bag she carried slapped against her leg. "You can't do that here. We'll get kicked out."

Lowering the sword, Lafitte met Juliet's green eyes. Anger burned inside him, but he realized his actions would draw unwanted attention. He expanded his chest with a full breath, then held it in. Through gritted teeth, he hissed, "She double-crossed me. I must avenge. I have waited two hundred years for this moment."

"You can, but without the sword." Juliet glanced around to make sure none of the other tourists in their group noticed the hot-tempered pirate. "I brought you here hoping you could find some answers. Legend has it that Marie Laveau haunts this cemetery." The bronze plaque on the lower left side of the tomb read: `This Greek Revival tomb is the reputed burial place of this notorious voodoo queen. A mystic cult, voodooism, of African origin, was brought to this city from Santo Domingo and flourished in the 19th century. Marie Laveau was the most widely known of many practitioners of the cult.`

Juliet looked around again, only finding the maze of mini mausoleums. The cemetery danced melodically between beauty and ruin. Weathered, macabre tombs told countless stories of the dead. They resembled small marbled houses that Mark Twain called "The City of the Dead."

The rest of the tour group moved on toward the tombs of the first governor of Louisiana William C.C. Claiborne and chess champion Paul Morphy. "Do you see her?" Juliet whispered and tugged on the hem of his voluminous sleeve.

"No," Lafitte answered with pursed lips. "But if I do, she is in for an affray." He reached for his sword again, but Juliet stopped him.

"You can't pull your sword out any time you want!"

"But I must avenge myself and my crew," he repeated.

"But not like that" Juliet sneered, hoping no one in their group saw him and helped Lafitte lower his sword.

"Maybe not now, but I swear that I shall."

Juliet glanced around them again. "But do you see anything else? Any clues to help you?"

Placing a hand on the graffitied tomb, Lafitte fell deep in thought. He closed his eyes and paused for a few moments. "No," he finally said.

"We can take a look around at the rest of the cemetery if you want."

"At this moment, I do not see anything that can assist me. I shall return when the sun has set."

"You can't. The cemetery's closed then. You'll get arrested if someone catches you."

"I witnessed other apparitions in the cemetery. But mourners dressed in black cannot help me. I must come up with another plan."

"Then let's get outta here. This place gives me the creeps, even in daylight." Juliet shuddered and headed toward the exit gate. Lafitte was on her heels.

They crossed the neutral ground at Basin again and headed one block toward the streetcar stop on North Rampart. Juliet pulled out her phone, clicked the Jazzy Pass app, and bought two one-way passes for $2.50. New Orleans was the first city west of the Allegheny Mountains to implement passenger rail service and still maintained low prices. It occurred to her that Jean Lafitte was old enough to get the senior rate of $0.40, but she had no way to prove his age.

They boarded the crowded streetcar and took a seat on one of the polished wooden benches. The old rail car click-clacked along the wide thoroughfare passing Congo Square and Louis Armstrong Park.

"Where are we headed?" Jean Lafitte asked Juliet.

"Back to my house." She sniffed at the air around him. "When was the last time you had a shower?"

"My regular bath was a week ago."

Juliet slapped a hand to her forehead.

Chapter 8

They arrived back at Juliet's house on Burgundy Street. Mrs. Hebert was still sitting on her porch next door.

"Who you got there with ya, Juliet?" she asked.

"Just a friend, Mrs. Hebert." She motioned to Jean Lafitte, hoping the old woman didn't ask too many questions. "He's in town for a coupla weeks. For Halloween."

"Oh, okay, sha." The neighborly woman stroked the dog on her lap as she smiled at her new acquaintance. "Welcome to New *OR-lens*."

"My pleasure." Jean Lafitte bowed deeply.

He and Juliet stepped into her house. This time, Juliet welcomed Lafitte in without fear. She had spent most of the day with a smug, obnoxious, swashbuckling Lothario, but he meant her no harm. She felt safe with him.

In the front room, she handed him the clothing bag and exchanged it for his red cloak. He removed his hat like a respectable gentleman. As she led him to her bathroom, she grabbed a fresh towel and washcloth from her linen closet.

He sniffed it and accidentally grazed her arm. "It smells like lavender. Like in the fields north of here."

"Yep."

In the bathroom, Juliet gave him quick instructions on how to use the toilet. "All of the stuff swirls down and out of sight."

Lafitte kneeled and gaped at the swirling water. "La vache!"

Then, Juliet opened the shower curtain and pulled the single knob to turn on the water. Lafitte stood to study the modern invention.

She said, "I'll set this for you, so don't touch it. When you're done, push this in. There's soap and shampoo in there for you. They're a little girly, but you'll smell better than you did." After wrinkling her nose, she reached in and handed him the bottle.

With curious intent, he inspected the cylindrical plastic container and turned it a few times on its sides.

"Here." Juliet stopped him and flipped open the cap. "Like this. Squeeze a small amount into your hand and then lather it in your hair." She set the bottle back in the shower.

"Aye. I thank you. You are a kind belle gosse." He tipped his chin at her.

"By the way, people nowadays take showers on a daily basis."

"Daily? A copper tub is not available every day for me. Baths take time and effort." His dark eyes grew round.

"Yes, daily. It's so much easier and faster now with a shower."

"What if I need assistance washing my back?" he asked with a seductive smile.

Juliet handed Lafitte a long-handled pouf that hung from a hook on the back shower tile. She realized he was more than hinting, but she refused to take the bait. Ignoring him, she said, "Leave your dirty clothes on the sink and I'll wash them."

"But they are of the finest silk and wool," Lafitte protested. "You shall need a quarter of a pound of honey, a quarter of a pound of soft soap, two wine glasses of gin, and three gills of boiling water."

"Umm." Juliet gave him a funny look. "I'll have them dry-cleaned." She thought about the money she had already spent on this guy. Hopefully, she would see a return. If everything he said was true, this could be an eventful next two weeks for her. The idea lifted her spirits from getting fired a few weeks earlier. "Give the water another minute to warm up and get in. Everything's here for you, so I'll be in the other room." Juliet slipped out the door and shut it behind her.

Jean Lafitte peeled off his boots and hat, then removed his breeches, stockings, and shirt. He laid them gently on the sink as he was instructed and ran his hand along the fine fabrics. The smooth material reminded him of Juliet's arm that he had lightly stroked moments before. He thought about other things he wished to do to her. She was a lovely and challenging beauty, unlike the easy trollops he was used to. But he had a treasure to find and a curse to break. His provocative thoughts and aching loins must wait.

Stepping into the shower, he gasped at the new sensation of beads of water hitting his bare skin. He had never felt a pulsating massage like this before, not even in the best brothels. The water cascaded down his body to the drain below. If he had one of these modern amenities on *The Pride,* he might never have left the ship. In front of him, foreign bottles of shampoo and body wash still puzzled him. He flipped the cap on one and inhaled. The scent of papaya enveloped him, reminding him of the beautiful women who offered him the luscious fruit on Isla Mujeres.

Twenty minutes later, Jean Lafitte emerged from the bathroom wearing jeans and a light blue hoodie. His thick black hair swept backward into damp waves. Now he was a couple of inches shorter in bare feet.

In the front room, Juliet sized him up with a smile. "Not bad. Do the boxers fit okay?" She sat on the couch and her laptop was open on the coffee table in front of her.

He wiggled his hips and adjusted his new jeans with his hands. "They are not silk, but they shall suffice."

"While you were in there, I did a little more research on Marie Laveau." She motioned for Lafitte to sit next to her. "Let me show you."

"What is this?" He reached for the images on Juliet's screen.

"It's a laptop. A computer." She was met with a blank stare. "It's like my phone I showed you earlier, but bigger and easier to read."

"Aye, I remember."

With deft fingers, Juliet brought up an online article. "It says here that Marie Laveau was a hair stylist for the wealthier families of New Orleans during the eighteen hundreds. She obtained inside information on her wealthy patrons by listening to ladies gossiping, or from their servants whom she either paid or cured of mysterious ailments. She used this information during her voodoo consultations with wealthy local women to enhance her image as a clairvoyant and used this intel to give them practical advice. She also made money by selling her clients gris-gris as charms to help their wishes come true." Juliet knocked her head from side to side. "Whether or not it's all true, I don't know."

"But she was the most powerful voodoo queen?" Lafitte inched closer to Juliet, squinting at the small type in front of them.

Juliet nodded. "That's what everyone says."

"The jewels gave her that power," Lafitte deduced.

"It's possible." Juliet shrugged. "Or she knew how to swindle people. Like a pirate."

"Touché."

Juliet continued, "It says she died in eighteen eighty-one, but her daughter kept the voodoo practice for several decades after."

"Interesting."

"Even today, she's an enigma." Juliet picked up her remote and turned on her TV. As she clicked on Hulu, Jean Lafitte's head jerked back.

"What is that?" His voice rose in pitch and he gawked at the people and sounds coming from the screen on the TV stand. He rose to explore it.

"It's a television."

"What is a television?" He edged closer to examine the large rectangle. Taking a step, he marveled at the back with interest. With a lingering touch, he furrowed his brows and released his fingers from the foreign object. He waved his hand behind the television, looking for a window. "We can see them, but they cannot see us?"

"Uh-huh." Juliet watched him intently; his curiosity about modern things intrigued her.

Still uncertain, Lafitte wrinkled his nose at the TV. "There is no window to another room?"

"Nope."

"I do not understand. But you can control it?"

"Yep, with this remote." Juliet held the piece out to him.

Hesitantly, he took it from her and sniffed it. Juliet laughed. He pressed a few buttons and immediately the channels changed and the volume blared. The noise from the TV was so loud, Juliet covered her ears. She swiped the remote out of Lafitte's hand and returned the TV to normal volume and back to Hulu.

"Check this out." Juliet found an episode of *American Horror Story*: *Coven* and a modern version of the voodoo queen appeared on the screen. "This show is a highly fictional version of Marie Laveau."

He gaped at the new sights and sounds coming from the television. He spoke slowly, still mesmerized, "Do you know if there is any word of the cursed jewels?"

"I had never heard that story until you told me."

Lafitte twirled his mustache between his fingers. "She kept them hidden because she did not want anyone to steal her power."

"Probably." Juliet rubbed her hands together.

"Women in voodoo did not have much power but they had *this* power. They danced naked in groups with serpents and were feared. Generating fear was powerful."

"Do you have any idea where the jewels could be now? Are you sure they're still in New Orleans?"

"I would assume her daughter kept them," Lafitte replied, his eyes bore into hers. "The jewels have to be here. They must be here. I cannot return to that purgatory."

"Why don't we take a ghost tour? It might give you some ideas." Juliet asked. "We can go tonight because I have to work tomorrow."

Chapter 9

At 8:00 that night, Juliet and Jean Lafitte joined twenty other people on the sidewalk outside of The Voodoo Lounge on North Rampart Street waiting to hear about disease, disaster, sinister spirits, and murder in The Crescent City. They all hoped to catch a glimpse of something supernatural in the city. Across the street, the archway to Armstrong Park lit up the area. As they waited for the tour guide to count attendees, Juliet peered at the dark October sky and leaned into Lafitte's ear. A few street lamps bounced shadows onto the surrounding buildings.

"Do you see anything up there?" She wasn't sure of anything anymore in the haunted city.

"Aye, some apparitions above the roofs and white specters against the brick." At the back of the group, Juliet followed his gaze even though she didn't see anything except unlit third-story balconies. "They are harmless," he added.

"If you see anything else, don't let anyone hear you," Juliet instructed. "You don't want to freak anyone out any more than they already are. You never know what people believe or don't believe."

Their guide, a sprite young woman with long blue hair in a flared dress covered with skeletons, introduced herself. "I'm Adelaide and I'll be takin' y'all around the French Quarter tonight." As she went over the rules of staying on the sidewalk and keeping with the group, Juliet took out her phone and snapped a few pictures. Even though she had lived in the city for eight years and knew the streets as well as anyone born here, she figured some photos could help them on their quest.

They traveled down Orleans Street stopping two blocks later for Adelaide to tell legendary stories of vampires in the city.

Lafitte scoffed under his breath. "What hornswoggle. Vampires are cheap imitations of thieves and murderers."

Adelaide heard his commotion in the back of the group. "Did you have something to add back there?"

Before Lafitte could run his mouth, Juliet clamped her hand over it. She spoke for him, "No, we're good."

Adelaide continued her stories.

Juliet warned Jean Lafitte, "I wouldn't say that too loud. Lots of people around here believe in vampires. You might find another hex on you."

"I have endured the hex of Marie Laveau. I am a seadog and can withstand anyone who wants to run a rig on me."

"Your funeral." Juliet didn't believe in vampires but anything was possible in this unique and magnetic city. "Do you have any ideas yet on how to find the jewels?"

"Aye."

After an awkward silent pause, Juliet asked, "Care to share?"

"A good captain does not share his plans until he knows for certain his crew can be trusted."

Juliet shook her head in annoyance and walked a few steps ahead of him.

Adelaide led the group toward Bourbon Orleans Hotel at the corner of Orleans and Bourbon Streets. Buildings that had snoozed during the day came alive with flamingo-colored neon signs. The crowd of tourists on the narrow sidewalk increased as they approached Halloween partiers downing hand grenade drinks from nearby Tropical Isle. In a bright green plastic yard cup, the potent drink was stronger than a hurricane and claimed to be the most powerful cocktail in New Orleans. Bringing up the rear, Juliet and Lafitte had trouble keeping up with their group because they had to navigate through and around the other folks on the sidewalk.

The group stopped in front of the grand green and white hotel with its plantation-style shutters and private wrought second-floor galleries, each secured by wrought-iron fencing.

"This hotel," Adelaide explained, "is haunted by a Confederate soldier on the sixth floor, a lonely dancer in the main ballroom, and several children and nuns who wander the floors."

Lafitte whispered in Juliet's ear, "I observe them in the windows. If I possessed my spyglass, I could tell you their intricacies."

Juliet smiled and let Adelaide finish her story.

Moments later, Adelaide guided the group toward Muriel's Restaurant at the edge of Jackson Square. "This is considered the most haunted restaurant in New Orleans," Adelaide began. "After the great fire of 1788 when 75% of the French Quarter burned down, Pierre Antoine Lepardi Jourdan purchased this piece of land to build a dream home for his family. Although he adored his beautiful house, he also had a penchant for gambling as many locals did back then. In 1814, he wagered his beloved home in a poker game and lost the one thing he treasured most in life. The shock of the loss was so intense that, before havin' to vacate the premises and hand over his treasure, he tragically committed suicide on the second floor right where Muriel's Séance Lounge is situated today."

The tour group gasped.

Adelaide gestured to the plexiglass window on the edge of the old building. "Jourdan's spirit still resides in Muriel's. Look in and see how the restaurant staff reserves a permanent VIP table for him. It is set with red wine and bread every night. As long as he is kept happy with wine and food, he won't cause mischief." Everyone gawked through the window at the roped-off table hoping to see the spirit of Pierre Jourdan.

"Do you see him?" Juliet asked Lafitte from the back of the group.

"Aye, he caught my eye and winked."

Juliet chuckled, unsure if she should believe him.

Adelaide made sure everyone had a chance to take photos. After the last picture was snapped, she steered the group northeast on Chartres Street. Chartres was pronounced "charters", another example of New Orleans' colorful words.

They dodged other partying tourists and made a right on St. Philip.

"I see the celebrations have not ended in this city," Lafitte noted.

"New Orleans is a nonstop party," Juliet said. "Everyone knows that."

"But do you know how it all originated?"

"Of course. Carnival from Rome and Venice." Juliet flashed him a look that said *duh*.

"Aye. And New Orleans hosted the first known St. Patrick's Day celebration in America in 1809--while I was ruling the bayou and streets. Then, forty years later, immigrants from Ireland fled the potato famine and arrived here."

Halfway down the block, Adelaide stopped the group in front of MRB Bar, an unassuming tan two-story building.

Lafitte talked low in Juliet's ear, "I passed this establishment last night on the way to my tavern. A young wench dressed like a witch spoke to me."

"Don't call women wenches," Juliet reprimanded him with a stern brow. "You might get slapped."

"Aye, I have many times. From the genteel ladies who flirted with their fans or dropped a handkerchief." Lafitte rubbed a hand against his cheek, remembering the stings from centuries ago. "What about strumpet?"

"No."

"Trollop?"

"No!"

Adelaide interrupted them and spoke to the group, "Everyone, we'll make a quick stop here if y'all need a break, but let me tell y'all the tale if y'all dare to enter." She pointed to the women in front of her. "Ladies, y'all listen up." The women in the group glanced at each other with an intrigued smirk. Adelaide continued, "Back in the 19th century, this strip of St. Philip was not the sort of place you wanted to visit if you had the opportunity to avoid it. One such woman was an Irish immigrant who arrived in New Orleans with great hope. Only, after realizin' that she had no resources to make it, she fell upon the oldest profession in the books: prostitution. She found employment at the brothel that used to be here at MRB."

A man piped up from the tour group, "What does MRB stand for?"

"Mississippi River Bar," Adelaide answered. "The Irish woman found love with one of her customers and the opportunity to get away from prostitution. He gave her many jewels and baubles as tokens of his affection. Then her beloved went off to war to earn money to marry her and returned in a pine box. She was devastated and hanged herself in the brothel's courtyard. Now it seems her spirit has never left and she is called The Lady of the Night. She is particularly fond of women with jewelry. She'll slip off rings, bracelets, necklaces, and earrings without the woman ever noticin'. She's also vindictive and jealous of any pretty woman in there. Women usin' the restroom have turned on the faucet to wash their hands. They glance up into the mirror, only to see an apparition of The Lady of the Night manifest right behind them. Before they have the chance to blink, their heads are smashed into the mirror." Adelaide locked eyes with Juliet, but spoke to the whole group. "Y'all can decide if y'all want to step inside or not."

Juliet fingered the silver bracelet around her wrist.

Jean Lafitte took notice of Juliet's trepidation and said, "She would take a liking to you. I shall protect you."

"Thanks," Juliet sarcassed. Even though she worked in a haunted tavern, she didn't want to risk losing the priceless bracelet that her mother gave her. She rolled her eyes at the unwanted chivalry and planted her feet firmly on the sidewalk. "But I'm good right here."

After other women in the group took their chances and ventured into the bar for a break, Adelaide led everyone to the next stop. They passed the haunted Hotel Provincial and the Old Ursuline Convent. Making a left on Governor Nicholls Street, a weathered cement wall on one side of the street surrounded them on one side and centuries-old Spanish-style homes on the other. Halloween decorations greeted them on all sides.

Adelaide walked backward as she addressed her group. "Do y'all smell the sweetness in the air?"

Several people nodded.

"That's the fig and orange trees brought over from Provence in the 1800s." She started to turn forward again but Jean Lafitte interrupted her.

"Aye, to cover the stench," he yelled from the back of the group.

Juliet shot him a look with daggers for eyes. "Stop it. You're gonna get us kicked out. You can't show up the tour guide."

"But she--"

Juliet shushed Lafitte and clamped a hand over his mouth.

"That's right," Adelaide agreed from the front. "In the early eighteen hundreds, the city's sewage system was so awful that the foul smell hovered stagnant in the air. The city officials got the trees to bring in a sweet scent." She swept her arms wide around her. "And a lot of those trees are still here today."

At the next block, Adelaide stopped the group at the corner of Governor Nicholls and Royal Streets. She herded the group in front of a one-story unpretentious building on the east side of the intersection, positioning her group under a set of street lamps. Keeping her back to the dark three-story Neoclassical building across the street, she took a deep breath and scraped a hand through her blue hair.

"Behind me," she gulped and cleared her throat, "is the LaLaurie Mansion. The most haunted buildin' in all of New Orleans. To tell y'all the truth, I hate comin' here. It gives me the creeps and I've heard multiple stories from other people who believe that this story I'm fixin' to tell y'all is true. Unlike Muriel's, this place has a sinister past. The legend is that if you walk under the second-story gallery--" Adelaide flicked a hand back without turning around, "-- you will be cursed. That's why we're stayin' right here."

A woman to Juliet's right spoke up, "This place was on *American Horror Story.*"

"Yep," Adelaide replied. "And it all starts with Madame Delphine LaLaurie." Adelaide told the tale of the French aristocrat's three doomed marriages and her mistreatment of slaves in the 1800s in the now-private home. "On the morning of April 10, 1834, a fire broke out at this luxurious house and destroyed the kitchen. When the fire department arrived, they found seven slaves who were starved, tortured, and chained in the upper part of the buildin'. The neighbors gathered outside and were horrified by the conditions. They formed an angry mob demandin' the head of the woman who did this."

"'Tis true," Lafitte whispered to Juliet in the back. "Creole women were more cruel to their slaves than men."

Juliet nodded solemnly.

Adelaide continued, "Madame Delphine LaLaurie escaped the fray and was never seen again. Allegedly, the fire was started on purpose by a slave woman chained to a stove as punishment. The fire seemed to be an attempt at tryin' to call attention to the deplorable conditions that she and her fellow slaves endured." Adelaide paused and blew out a deep sigh. "The mansion has changed hands over the years and every owner has come face to face with some kind of tragedy. In 2009, actor Nicholas Cage bought the property. Soon after, his movie career took a nosedive. Coincidence? Some of this story has been disputed over the years claimin' facts have been fabricated, but a friend of mine had the opportunity to go inside the mansion last year. When he returned, he had claw marks down his back."

Juliet gasped and clamped a hand over her mouth. She had heard similar stories about the building but nothing so specific. She turned to find Jean Lafitte studying the inky sky. His lips parted, and he twirled his mustache between his fingers.

"What is it?" Juliet whispered.

"I see three white orbs moving in front of the mansion." He pointed toward the massive palladium windows on the third floor. He watched them with a discerning eye.

"I don't see them."

Placing one hand on Juliet's shoulder, Lafitte drew her attention up toward the roof with his other hand. "There."

A shudder spread through Juliet's body. The three orbs appeared in the sky to her. She drew her mouth into a straight line and chewed her bottom lip. Since he touched her, did that mean she could now see what he saw in the City of the Dead?

"I see them," Juliet squealed through a whisper. She didn't want to alarm the others in their group of her mystical revelation. "When you put your hand on me, they appeared."

"Bloody hell." Lafitte lifted his hand from her shoulder and the orbs disappeared from her sight. He touched and released her several times, each instance the orbs appeared and reappeared to Juliet.

"This is awesome," Juliet whispered. Intrigue mixed with a slight amount of fear surged through her. The City of the Dead brought on a whole new meaning for her.

Chapter 10

Later that night, as Juliet set up bedding on her couch for Jean Lafitte, she asked, "Did you get any ideas tonight where to look for the jewels?" Her blonde hair was loosely pulled up into a topknot on her head. She wore a silky pajama pants set and he stood wearing his new sweatpants and an oversized Baltimore Ravens T-shirt Juliet had lent him.

"Aye. Two hundred years has given me plenty of time to seek revenge to gain salvation. Most of the buildings are the same as when they were when my brother Pierre and I ruled New Orleans. If my memory has not left me, then I shall still be able to find my way around. I had spies everywhere. In saloons, shops, and brothels. But without my men, it may be more difficult. I will need to find an able-bodied crew on land. Now that I can communicate with the spirits who have never left, I shall question them about Marie Laveau and her daughter. Perhaps they can assist."

"And I can see them as long as you touch me," Juliet added. She stood upright to face him, his six-foot frame towered over her.

He reached for her cheek. That kind and lovely face was inches from him.

Juliet jerked back, out of his grasp. "Don't even think about it! I meant my arm or shoulder."

"My apologies, belle gosse." However, he cocked his head to the side and a smirk formed on his lips, his smug expression did not match his words.

"Just so we're clear. This..." Juliet flicked a hand back and forth between her and Jean Lafitte. "...is not gonna happen. You might've bedded every woman in New Orleans 200 years ago, but I'm not falling for your easy lines." Getting involved with someone, especially a known raunchy pirate, for two weeks did not interest her.

"How are you not attracted to Captain Jean Lafitte?" The edge of his mouth curved into a sly grin. "Besides gambling and drinking, wenches are a vice. They swoon in my presence and are honored to be with me."

SMACK! Juliet's hand slapped against his face. "I warned you not to call us wenches. I am a *woman.*"

Rubbing his hand over his cheek, he soothed the sting. "Proper women require chaperones and you do not have one," he countered. As he glanced about the empty room, his eyes darkened. "You reside alone in this house. No man is here. Your virtue must be questionable."

"My virtue?" Juliet clapped back. Now he was insulting her.

"Aye, since you deny me, you must be a prude." He motioned to her modern pajama pants set. "Nor do you wear long white night clothes."

Juliet laughed out loud. No one had ever called her a prude before. The number of lovers in her relationship scrapbook was enough to know what she liked in bed. But it wasn't so long that she forgot their names.

"I'm not a prude," Juliet chuckled through her teeth. "But you can't assume every woman wants to sleep with you. We aren't at your beck and call saying 'Aye, Aye, Captain.'" She mock-saluted him.

"But the wen--, er women, I have observed on Bourbon Street since I have arrived on land are loose and imbibe on your rum," he countered. "Surely, I could bed them."

"But you still have to ask for consent. If she says no, you leave her alone. You can't assume you know what she wants." She knew he wouldn't know the old saying that to "assume" makes an "ass out of you and me." "And you can't steal women either. You'll go to jail. The laws are different now."

"But I am a pirate. Thievery is my birthright."

"Women are off limits. Don't do it." She shook a finger at him. "Women have come a long way since your time. We live alone. We own businesses. We vote. We drive. We walk by ourselves without your chaperones." A chuckle slipped out at her last statement because she had never heard of anything so absurd. She bit her lip to hide a smile. "We wear pants and--" she covered her mouth with her hand and faked a gasp. "We even show our ankles."

"You are mocking me." His initial agitation turned to amusement. His face reddened then turned a shiny pink.

Juliet nodded and stifled a laugh. "Yes, I am."

"Well done, belle gosse. It is not often that someone bests me."

"We good now?" Juliet bent to smooth the blankets on the couch.

"Good?" Lafitte tilted his head in confusion.

She stood upright again and snapped her finger a few times trying to think. "You know... are we... what's your word that's opposite of enemies?"

"Hearties."

"Yes, hearties." Juliet offered her hand to seal the deal.

"Aye, hearties." Lafitte spit into his right hand then shook hers with exerted effort.

Juliet cringed at his grossness but nodded in agreement.

"You hungry?" She walked toward her kitchen. "I have some leftover bread pudding in the fridge."

"What is a fridge?" Lafitte stayed on her heels.

Without answering, Juliet opened the refrigerator door and Jean Lafitte shielded his eye from the glaring light. She laughed at his out-of-date reaction. "Don't worry, it's harmless." She reached inside and pulled out a glass container full of the bread, egg, and cream concoction. When she shut the fridge door and stepped toward the center island, Lafitte opened the fridge again to check out the light.

"How does it work?" He opened and closed the door many times, gaping at the light beam turning on and off before the fridge sealed shut.

Laughing, Juliet held the door open and pressed the small white button on the inside of the fridge. The light turned off. When she released it, the light turned back on.

"La vache," Lafitte gasped.

"Not only does it have a light, it can keep food cold indefinitely."

"My crew tossed spoiled food overboard to the fish."

"We don't have to do that anymore." Juliet went to her cabinets and grabbed two bowls and forks. From another container, Juliet drizzled hot buttered rum sauce on top of the bread pudding. She warmed both bowls in her microwave as Jean Lafitte watched with unbridled curiosity.

"How did it do that?" he asked. He cautiously raised a hand over the steaming dessert. "Moments ago, they were cold."

"The microwave is a modern invention. Makes reheating on a stove--or fire--obsolete."

He huffed at her with admiration.

With a point of pride, she presented her favorite dessert to him. "*Bon appétit.*"

"*Merci, ça a l'air merveilleux.*" Lafitte came face to face with her blank look.

"Sorry, I don't speak French," Juliet confessed. She forked a piece of bread pudding and took a bite.

"But you just said *bon appétit.*"

"Most chefs say that nowadays when they offer their food."

"I said 'This looks wonderful.'" He took a bite and smiled wide. "It *is* wonderful. I can taste the rum."

"I always add a little extra." Juliet winked at him. "We call it *lagniappe.*"

"I would pay a hundred doubloons for this."

"That's the plan. I want to open my own bakery. I can't tend bar forever."

"What is prohibiting you?"

"Don't have the funds." Juliet frowned.

"Steal them. When my gold and rum were low, I found a new supply on other ships."

"I'm not stealing anything." Juliet vigorously shook her head at him.

"Very well, your choice." Lafitte ate another piece of bread pudding. "Where did you learn to cook?"

"My mother owned a bakery in Baltimore and she taught me." She gestured to the Ravens T-shirt he wore.

"My compliments to your mother." He swallowed another bite. "I shall like to tell her myself."

"She passed away ten years ago," Juliet replied. "My father, too."

"My condolences." Lafitte placed his fork on the island, stepped back, and bowed.

"Thank you." She offered him a weak smile. "How long did you live in France?"

"I was born in Bordeaux and spent my first twenty years aboard ships owned by my father who was a trader. This was where I learned to love the seas. My native language is French, then I learned Spanish and eventually English."

"Perfect for New Orleans. The city is full of those ethnicities."

"Aye, when my brother Pierre and I were here two hundred years ago, France gave up control of Louisiana to Spain from 1763 until 1803 to pay a war debt. Several fires destroyed New Orleans' original French architecture during Spain's 40-year rule, and, as I saw tonight on our tour, many of the remaining buildings have Spanish influence. The flat-tiled roofs, tropical colors, and ornate ironwork are Iberian touches brought from across the Atlantic. To prevent more fires, the

Spanish-controlled government mandated that stucco replace wood for construction and that all buildings be placed close together and near the street. Where there used to be front yards and open spaces surrounding buildings, the French Quarter was now rendered both more intimate and secretive, with continuous façades, arched passageways, and splendid rear gardens and courtyards hidden from public view. In a twist of events, this created more hiding places for my lawless associates."

"It's funny you remember all that." Juliet slid another bite of bread pudding into her mouth.

"When you are banished to a ship for two centuries, the mind remembers marvelous things."

Juliet laughed out loud.

"Where can I acquire gunpowder?" Lafitte took the last bite of his bread pudding. "Is there an alchemist nearby?"

"Gunpowder?" Juliet choked on the last of her dessert.

"Aye, gunpowder to fill my pistol. I shall need to keep it dry or it will be useless."

Juliet glared at him. "You don't need your pistol. Most people around here are happy to help. Though I know a bunch of people whose car got broken into. We believe everyone should have a good time. Despite the crime, most people are friendly around here. The locals, at least. Lots of tourists are self-centered and entitled. I try to avoid them."

"Then I need my pistol," Lafitte pointed out. "To ward off the entitled tourists, as you say."

"No, you don't. They have bad attitudes, but they're harmless. Besides, if you wave your gun at someone, you'll get arrested. You can't even carry your gun. I told you the laws are different now."

"Interesting." As he sat at the island, Lafitte twirled his mustache between his fingers.

"I need to get to bed now. I have to work tomorrow morning." She grabbed their empty plates and put them in the sink. "The couch is all set up for you." She headed for the doorway and turned back to face him. "Good night, Captain."

Jean Lafitte stood from his stool and bowed deeply. "You have been most hospitable, belle gosse."

Chapter 11

The next morning, Juliet found Jean Lafitte dressed in his silk shirt and breeches standing in her front room. His leather boots leaned against her wall. "You don't like the clothes I bought you?"

He smoothed the silk against his skin. "I prefer my own."

"Whatever you want." Juliet shrugged and grabbed a jean jacket from her coat rack. The October weather in New Orleans could be as cool as 60 or as warm as 80. She threw the jacket over a Ramones T-shirt. Black low-top Chuck Taylors were on her feet. "I'm going to work now. You'll stay here until I get back later this afternoon. Let me give you a quick rundown of everything."

For the next 15 minutes, Juliet showed Jean Lafitte how to operate the TV, microwave, sink, and lights. "You don't need to touch the stove or washing machine," she told him. "Help yourself to anything in the kitchen. If anyone comes to the door, don't answer it. I don't need my neighbors asking questions about you. I still can't believe this all myself…"

"Aye." He stood next to her at the front door.

"Okay, I think that's all. Stay here and we'll work on your treasure hunt tonight. And don't go in my bedroom." He nodded and she opened the door to leave. "See you later."

"Farewell, belle gosse."

Juliet left Jean Lafitte locked in her house and walked to the tavern with his namesake. She hoped he didn't find the jewelry on her dresser. After all, gold was his vice. Too late now. She had to trust him.

Even with all the weirdness around her, Juliet truly loved her adopted city. The *joie de vivre* beckoned her. New Orleans beckoned with her expansive palette, love for life, and grit. Juliet soon fell in love with everything she never knew she wanted. She devoured the jambalaya, gumbo, and collard greens. The vibrant yet unique city pulled Juliet into its clutches one bite at a time. She missed the colors of autumn in Maryland, farm stands full of pumpkins, and even snow, but New Orleans was heartbreakingly beautiful and full of life. She couldn't imagine living anywhere else.

Soon, she stepped through the wooden doors at Lafitte's Blacksmith Shop Bar and found Leah stringing gauze spider webs around the brick fireplace in the center of the room. Sunlight poured in through the windows giving it an ethereal glow.

"Hey, Jules."

"Hey, girl," Juliet said. "You wouldn't believe my last thirty-six hours. Hell, I'm not sure if I believe it."

Leah handed her a strand of gauze. "Help me out and fill me in."

For the next fifteen minutes, while they decorated the rest of the tavern, Juliet told Leah about her new house guest, the curse, and her latest ability to see apparitions.

"Whoa!" Leah gasped. "You can see ghosts now? Like for real?"

"Yeah, it's weird." Juliet raked a hand through her blonde hair. "I'm a little freaked out, but oddly intrigued. I can only see them if Jean Lafitte is touching me though. I can see things floating through the air and apparitions wandering the streets as if they belong there."

"You could totally mess with the ghost tour guides," Leah laughed. "What did you see? What did they do?"

"Three giant orbs floating above the LaLaurie Mansion. It was cool, but terrifying. I can't even describe it."

"You could totally cash in on this. Post stories on Instagram and everythin'."

"Eh. Maybe? It might have been a one-off. Who knows if it will happen again."

When the friends were done, fake spider webs stretched across the bar and through the rafters. Orange blinking lights illuminated the place. Perfect for Halloween.

"What'll you two do tonight?" Leah asked.

"No idea," Juliet replied. "I'm sure he'll come up with a plan. He's been stewing on a boat for two hundred years. I'm sure he has some ideas."

"But you're not scared of him? After all, he's a pirate. They pillage and set things on fire." Leah restocked some plastic cups for the Purple Drank. "Hide your good jewelry."

"Oddly, I'm not afraid. He's been a gentleman most of the time. Except when I slapped him for calling women wenches."

"Good for you," Leah chuckled.

At 10:00, customers searching for a liquid breakfast entered the bar and settled at a table.

"I got 'em," Juliet said.

* * * *

At Juliet's house, Jean Lafitte explored his surroundings. The books on her bookcase had odd covers and titles. He didn't understand all of the candles she owned. If she had electricity, why did she need them? Even though she taught him how to use the kitchen sink, the faucet still fascinated him. On and off, on and off, the water flowed in spurts.

Juliet had been gone for a few hours and Jean Lafitte found morning television boring. He didn't understand people sitting around on chairs talking or contestants guessing words for money. Restlessness overcame him. After inspecting his sword and pistol, his chores were done. He shifted from the front room to the kitchen and back again, checking the front windows for interesting activity every time. After a few tries, he figured out how to brew himself some coffee. The potency was different from what he was used to, but he still enjoyed it as the warm, chicory flavor filled his nostrils. He moaned in delight. Lafitte sat at Juliet's island, tapping his boots on the wooden floor. His patience was running out. Two centuries on *The Pride* was long enough. He needed to get out of the house, into the streets, into the city he had watched for the last 200 years. He had to find the cursed jewels. If he didn't, he and his crew would be banished to the river forever. He couldn't wait for Juliet.

Minutes later, Jean Lafitte made his way through the Marigny, taking a right on Royal Street, and faced Esplanade. Cars and trucks sped across the boulevard in front of him, like salmon swimming in schools. Remembering how Juliet had taught him how to stop at the red light, he waited to cross the neutral ground. Oak trees stretched upward casting dark shadows on the ground. As a fall breeze picked up, he held his tricorn hat to his head. He was on a determined mission.

When the crosswalk signal turned white, Jean Lafitte crossed Esplanade and a few passersby joined him. "Nice Halloween costume," a middle-aged woman said to him. "You look better than Jack Sparrow. And the rest of your crew too."

"Hmph," Lafitte huffed. "I certainly hope so."

He sauntered down Royal Street and realized he needed to cover ground faster. He needed to get to his old haunts and find the missing jewels. The French Quarter spread out in front of him and he had several stops to make. Then he noticed the old black horse tethering posts still cemented along the block.

That gave him an idea.

Chapter 12

Jean Lafitte found himself on the southeast side of Jackson Square. Across the green park, St. Louis Cathedral towered into the sky. Above the dark spires, Lafitte watched black spirits circling the haunted church.

"They are useless to me," he muttered to himself. "If I were on *The Pride*, they could serve as her lookout, but that is all."

Playfully, Jean Lafitte rattled the tip of his sheathed sword against the vertical rails of the black wrought iron fence that surrounded Jackson Square. He stopped at Decatur where tour guides hitched their mule-drawn carriages. Unexpectedly, the last carriage in the row was led by a brown horse. Mules fared better in the heat, so seeing the horse was a pleasant surprise for Lafitte. As the tour guide took a break at a nearby Lucky Dog vendor, Lafitte eyed the network of straps that connected the horse to the carriage that had a single bench seat for passengers. He considered cutting the horse free. His gold-handled cutlass was no match for the thick leather straps if he wanted a fast getaway. Not to be deterred, Lafitte swiftly jumped onto the driver's seat and snapped the reins at the horse.

"Hi-yah!" he called. The horse's ears flicked back and forth for a moment, hesitant of the new driver. Lafitte slapped the long reins on the gelding's rump. The animal sensed the human's confidence and took off. The tour guide yelled after him, running behind to no avail.

The horse galloped down Decatur with Jean Lafitte steering it away from cars and motorcycles. At the next intersection, Lafitte commanded the horse right on Toulouse Street. Not knowing it was a one-way street, cars slammed their brakes on the narrow street coming head to head with the carriage. Unlike the five-lane avenues in Manhattan, the Deep South street had zero forgiveness.

He tugged on the reins. "Whoa!" Lafitte shouted but the horse barely slowed. He pulled a couple more times and then applied the hand brake. Slowing down, the horse hopped the sidewalk in front of New Orleans Creole Cookery. People dodged the horse and scattered. Lafitte had the horse cut across to Chartres through a parking lot. Not knowing he was on another one-way street, Lafitte swerved the horse around oncoming traffic and faced a new stream of cars head-on. He reached for the hand brake again and screeched to a halt. They jumped the sidewalk once more, leaving knocked-over trash cans in their wake. A half block later, Lafitte aimed the horse and carriage toward St. Louis Street. Finally, they were going with traffic instead of against it. Lafitte slowed the horse to a trot.

Guiding the horse and carriage around the perimeter of the pretentious marbled Louisiana Court House, Lafitte was determined to find some answers in The Quarter. If nothing else, he needed a new able-bodied crew since his men were stuck on the ship.

He steered the horse to make a left on Royal and maintained speed with the rest of the traffic on the street known for its haughty antique shops. The buildings around him had a familiar yet peculiar look to him. The original Spanish and French candy-colored architecture was now modernized with new signage, updated furniture on the second-story balconies, and electric lighting where gas lamps once were. A combination of comfort and intrigue filled Lafitte. The rumbling cars and delivery trucks fascinated him.

Before Lafitte could pursue his destination and search for familiar contacts, he had a quick stop to make to empty his full bladder. If memory served him right, he could make a left onto Conti Street and find an alley to do his business. He guided the horse onto Conti with the black iron fence surrounding the courthouse on his left. Giant palm trees surrounding the law building cast shade onto the street. He passed two buildings that snuggled next to each other and then made a quick right into the alley snuggled between peach and yellow buildings.

Parking the horse along the side of the orange-colored restaurant, Lafitte hopped off the carriage, leaned against the brick wall, and lowered his breeches.

As he was finishing up, the click-clacking of someone's shoes against the sidewalk caught his attention. The person stepped closer to Lafitte.

"Hey there," the man said and Lafitte finally looked up. The man was wearing a dark blue short-sleeved shirt and matching pants. Tattoos inked their way up his left arm. A silver star inscribed with "New Orleans Police" was affixed to the left breast of his shirt. A walkie-talkie encircled his neck. "E. Martinez Task Police" was stitched into the right side of his uniform top.

Lafitte gawked at him, startled that he was interrupted. The horse snorted behind him.

"You can't be urinating in a public alley," the police officer said.

"Why not?" Lafitte shot back. "I have done it before without issue."

Officer Martinez chuckled at the unexpected response, but quickly recovered. "Because it's against the law." He pulled a small notepad from his hip pocket.

Before the police officer could write a ticket, they were interrupted by the carriage driver who ran at them, out of breath. He wiped the sweat from his brow and gasped for air. "There's the man who stole my horse!"

Officer Martinez glanced at the man, at Lafitte, at the horse and carriage, and back at the driver. "This man stole your horse?"

"Yes!" He reached for his carriage permit in his pants pocket and handed it to the police officer. "This is my horse and carriage."

Lafitte gaped at them, with arrogance. He was a pirate who got what he wanted, without letting an incompetent carriage driver stand in his way.

The driver strode over to his horse and stroked the gelding's nose. "Everythin'll be okay. I'm here."

"Stealing a horse..." Officer Martinez nodded his head toward Lafitte. "That's a felony. Turn around and put your hands behind your back."

"What?" Lafitte dropped his jaw at the officer.

"Let's go, pal." Officer Martinez flicked his hand at Lafitte to speed things up and pushed him against the side of the building. "You're under arrest for stealing a horse." With his other hand, he yanked handcuffs from his belt.

Before Officer Martinez could slap handcuffs on Lafitte, Lafitte pulled his pistol from his sash and raised it in front of the officer.

In an instant, Officer Martinez jerked his gun from his holster and aimed it at Lafitte. "Put the weapon down!" he commanded. "Let's make this easy for all of us." The driver cowered behind them, shielded by his carriage.

"I am Jean Lafitte the Pirate," Lafitte bellowed, without lowering his pistol. "I will defend myself by any means possible."

"Lower your weapon," Officer Martinez instructed through gritted teeth. His gun was aimed at Lafitte's head. "I won't tell you again."

Suddenly, the horse snorted again, causing Lafitte to lose his concentration and turn his head toward the carriage.

Without missing a beat, Officer Martinez knocked Lafitte's pistol out of his hand and it clanked to the sidewalk. He grabbed Lafitte's arms, twisting them behind him, and slapped handcuffs on his wrists. Gripping Lafitte with one hand, he picked up the pistol with his other hand and pushed him out of the alley and onto Conti Street. As Lafitte struggled to break free, Officer Martinez clutched him tighter and led him off. The driver mounted his carriage and followed them.

"I am Captain Jean Lafitte! Remove your hands from me!"

"Shut up!" Officer Martinez shouted. "You have the right to remain silent. Anything you say can and will be used against you in a court of law. You have the right to speak to an attorney, and to have an attorney present during any questioning. Do you understand these rights?"

Lafitte nodded with a suspicious eye, finally remaining quiet. He remembered that if he continued to fight, he might be hanged in Jackson Square. Thieves were hanged. Especially pirate thieves.

A half block later, Officer Martinez pushed Lafitte through the doors of the New Orleans Police Department.

Chapter 13

The phone at Lafitte's Blacksmith Shop rang a few times before anyone picked it up. Juliet and Leah hustled back and forth from the bar serving drinks to locals and tourists. Customers laughed and relaxed around the bar, downing the Purple Drank.

After the fifth ring, Juliet caught her breath enough to answer the phone. "Hello, Lafitte's."

"I'm looking for a woman named Juliet," the man on the phone said.

"This is her."

"This is Officer Martinez with the NOPD. I have someone in custody who says he knows you and needs your help."

Juliet's shoulders slumped and she gasped quietly. "What? Who?" Her mind went blank thinking of who could need her help. She didn't know any criminals. Then she remembered who she left at her house that morning. "Oh, no..." she muttered.

"He says his name is Jean Lafitte. He had no ID on him and no other effects except for a gold-handled sword and a pistol. Do you know him?"

"Yes. Yes, I do."

"Can you come to the police station and help us sort this out?"

"I'll be right there."

After Juliet quickly explained to Leah what was going on and grabbed her purse, she rushed through the French Quarter. She wasn't sure how to describe her relationship with Jean Lafitte to the police. Should she say he was a relative of hers with mental issues? That was probably not a good idea. Should she tell them the truth? They would laugh at her. But then again, the city was full of delusional people and they probably heard it all.

At 12:30, she found herself at the New Orleans Police Department. Inside the yellow two-story building, a clerk buzzed Juliet into the waiting room. City, state, and national flags perched on a high wall. Rotary Club plaques decorated an opposite wall. A few other people shifted in their seats. Juliet heard officers down the hall discussing cases. Phones rang and doors buzzed deeper in the building. Dispatchers spoke quietly into their headphones and created a murmur.

A moment later, Officer Martinez stood in front of her, his thumbs hooked through the belt loops on his pants. He stood a head taller than her and his muscles bulged through his sleeves. His face belonged on the cover of a magazine. She found him incredibly attractive. Under other circumstances, Juliet would have liked to get to know him better.

"I'm Juliet Vance. You called me about my friend."

"Glad you're here. Can I get you some coffee?" he offered.

"No, thanks. I'm good."

"It's probably for the best. It's gray and has a weird smell to it."

She choked on a laugh but didn't want to bother with chitchat, at least not then. "You have Jean Lafitte in custody?" Her voice cracked.

"Yes, ma'am. He's in lockup."

"What did he do?"

"Stole a horse, for one. Resisted arrest. Public urination. And assaulted an officer with a deadly weapon."

"Holy crap!" Juliet cupped a hand to her mouth. "I left him at my house this morning and he did all that in a few hours?"

"Apparently." Officer Martinez cocked his head at her. "But he says his name is Jean Lafitte. As I said on the phone, he had no ID on him. When we offered him his one phone call, he had no idea how to use a phone. When we asked him who we could call for him, he said you at his blacksmith bar. That's all he could tell us." He lowered his chin at her. "Does he have mental issues?"

Juliet chuckled for the second time since she got the unexpected call. "No, if only that were the case."

"Then who is he? He *seemed* lucid and sure of himself as if I was the one in the wrong."

Juliet sighed deeply. "You wouldn't believe me if I told you."

"Try me. I've seen enough in this city that could blow your mind. Last week was Friday the 13th and our lockup was filled with crazies. Some guy howlin' at the moon thinkin' he was a werewolf. A bunch of wanna-be vampires who tried to sacrifice a dog. This is New Orleans after all. Being a little nutty comes with the territory."

Juliet sighed again. "He has no ID because he really is Jean Lafitte the Pirate."

"What?" Officer Martinez gawked at her and wiped his forehead. "That's a new one."

"I'm telling you the truth. Two nights ago, he showed up at the bar where I work looking for his cursed jewels."

"Cursed jewels?" Officer Martinez arched an eyebrow at her. "For real?"

She wondered if he thought she was crazy, too.

"Yes, cursed jewels. He told me how he's been hexed to his ship on the Mississippi for the past two hundred years because one of his crew members stole jewels from Isla Mujeres in Mexico and Marie Laveau double-crossed him and swiped the jewels from him and that's how she got her power." Juliet took a breath from talking so fast.

"Marie Laveau the voodoo queen?" He smirked at her as if she had three heads. "The real Marie Laveau?"

"Yes." Juliet shuffled her feet back and forth. "I told you you wouldn't believe me."

"No, it's just..." Officer Martinez gazed over Juliet's head, trying to come up with a reasonable explanation. "Let's say all of this is true. He still stole a horse, assaulted me with his pistol, took a piss in an alley, and resisted arrest."

"So, he has to stay in jail?"

"Unless you want to bail him out?"

A small moan escaped Juliet's lips. "How much?"

"That's up to the bail officer to tell you, but I'm guessing around seven fifty."

"Fine." She rolled her eyes as she thought about the meager amount of savings she had in her bank account. "Can I see him?"

"Sure, but he has to stay behind bars until he's bailed out."

Officer Martinez buzzed Juliet through secure doors and into a long hallway that led to the prison cells. He gestured to the last cell at the end of the large sterile room. Iron bars stretched from floor to ceiling. Juliet gulped hard as she stepped closer to the human cage. A wooden bench was secured to the floor and graffiti was etched into the cement wall. The stale stench of sweat and mildew was enough to make her gag. Even though Juliet was only a visitor, the prison cell made her uneasy.

"Lafitte, you have a visitor," Officer Martinez yelled into the cell full of a half dozen criminals. Cat calls whistled out of the mouths of the other miscreants as Jean Lafitte made his way toward the front, his cloak sashaying as he walked.

"Release me from this atrocity." He gripped the iron bars. "I cannot stay in gaol."

"It'll cost me a lot of money if I get you out."

One of the other felons approached them from behind Jean Lafitte. His clothes were tattered and he reeked of urine and beer. "Who's your girlfriend, Jack Sparrow?"

"Leave her alone," Lafitte sneered, not looking at the unkempt convict.

Officer Martinez marched forward in a silent warning. He tapped the top of his billy club and the man stepped back.

Lafitte spoke again to Juliet, "I promise you that I shall make it up to you."

"But you said earlier you don't trust me." She crossed her arms over her chest.

"Please," he breathed out. "I cannot waste more time. I need your help. It is not often that I give my word, but when I do, I am good for it. I promise you. You have my word."

Juliet stared at him and pursed her lips in thought. He needed a lot of her money. Should she trust a pirate that she'll get it back? Pirates had a reputation to steal, lie, and cheat. How could she know if he was telling the truth or not?

She shook her head and puffed out a disgruntled sigh. "Fine. I'll get you out of here."

"You are my new First Mate." A small smile formed on his lips.

Officer Martinez interrupted them and spoke to Juliet, "I can take you over to the bail officer then I'll bring him up to you in the waiting room once everything is processed. Since he has no ID, you'll have to vouch for him and sign a statement that he is who you say he is. They'll probably copy your license."

"Okay, thanks." Juliet blew out another disgruntled sigh.

A few minutes later, Juliet stood in front of the bail officer. The older woman seemed bored as if she was counting the days until her retirement. A piece of plexiglass separated them. Juliet spoke to her through a round metal intercom.

The woman said, "The total fines are as follows: five hundred for public urination, five hundred for resisting arrest, one thousand for stealing a horse. And five thousand for assault with a deadly weapon."

Juliet's stomach dropped and a vein throbbed in her forehead.

The bail processor spoke again, her voice stoic, "Bail payment is ten percent. That'll be seven hundred dollars to bail out Jean Lafitte."

"Oh...kay." Juliet grimaced at the large amount of money. She pulled out her credit card and slid it through the hole in the base of the plexiglass at the desk. That kind of money put a dent in her savings. Jean Lafitte owed her. He owed her big.

Without emotion, the woman ran up Juliet's credit card. Then she pushed some papers and a well-worn pen through the base like a robot. "Sign these. They're an acknowledgment statement that you confirm his identity. Initial at the bottom of each page and sign the last one." Her dryness compared to the Sahara. "I'll need to copy your license."

Juliet quickly signed the paperwork and handed them and her license to the woman.

"His arraignment will be held in Courtroom 1 on Friday, October 27th at 10:00 in the mornin'," the woman spoke without making eye contact. She exchanged Juliet's credit card with paperwork. "Make sure he's here at that time. Since he assaulted the officer with a gun, that weapon has been confiscated until his hearin'. The rest of his personal effects can be claimed at this time. A public defender will be assigned to him unless you're payin' for an attorney too."

"No, ma'am." Usually, Juliet could make anyone crack a smile. Not this time.

"That's fine. If he doesn't show, you'll lose the money you're payin' today." She copied Juliet's license in a small black machine and set it in the plexiglass hole.

"Yes, ma'am. I'll make sure he's here."

Chapter 14

After Officer Martinez brought Jean Lafitte up from lockup, the police returned his sword to him. Juliet quickly ushered him out of the police station. Only Lafitte's pistol remained behind. They stopped on the sidewalk on Royal Street in front of the police station, finally out of earshot of the police officers. Tourists wandered by them, blithely ignoring Juliet conversing with a man dressed like a pirate. The sweet scent of azaleas filled the air around them.

"You stole a horse!" Juliet stabbed a finger at him. "What were you thinking?"

"I needed to get around town quickly. T'was the fastest way I knew."

"You can't steal a horse!" she spat. Her face flushed with fury. "And you had your gun on you! I told you the laws are different now."

"I do not go anywhere without my pistol. And you said I could not steal women. You did not state anything about a horse." He glared at her, hands on hips.

Juliet slapped a hand to her forehead. "You can't steal *anything*. A horse. A woman. Nothing." The veins in her neck throbbed and frustration filled her. "And now you lost your gun."

He sighed in defeat, something he rarely did. "Very well. I am forever in your debt, belle gosse."

"You're damn right you are! You cost me seven hundred dollars!" Juliet wanted to yank up the black iron fencing nearby and stab Jean Lafitte with it.

"Only seven hundred?" Amused, he twirled his mustache between his fingers. "Governor Claiborne put a bounty on my head for that much money for my capture. I thumbed my nose at him by parading through New Orleans arm in arm with my brother. But then I offered a *five thousand dollar* reward for the abduction of the governor." He chuckled, remembering the event.

"You can't do that either! There are no rewards or bounties anymore. Seven hundred dollars is a lot of money for someone who doesn't *steal* it!" Juliet snapped, her green eyes bore into him like daggers. "It's not like I have gold doubloons stashed away in my house."

"We can remedy that when I find the jewels."

"When *we* find the jewels," Juliet corrected him. "You aren't going anywhere without me. Not after the stunt you pulled today. I don't have any more money to bail you out of jail. You owe me."

"Indeed, I do. I am in your debt. Without you, I may have ended up hanged in Jackson Square."

"No one gets hanged in Jackson Square anymore."

"Then I would have been tar and feathered."

Juliet shook her head. "Nope, don't do that anymore either."

"Good thing I had my sword to protect myself from that constable."

"Yeah, but he had a gun."

"As did I, but I am a master swordsman," Lafitte countered. "'Tis why I lived as long as I have."

"A gun beats a sword every time. Like in *Raiders of the Lost Ark*." A joking smile formed on Juliet's mouth.

"What?" He gaped at her, unfamiliar with the reference.

"Never mind." She shook her head and glanced at her phone. Two hours had passed since she left work. "I need to get back to the bar." She grabbed him by the arm. "And you're coming with me."

Mid-afternoon, they walked through the open doors at Lafitte's Blacksmith Shop Bar. Leah was behind the bar and Derek was delivering drinks to customers.

"Look who's back," Leah called to Juliet and Jean Lafitte above the noise of the crowd. "Everything okay, Jules?"

"I'm out seven hundred dollars because this guy stole a horse and threatened an NOPD Officer with his pistol." With an eye roll, she shoved Lafitte onto a stool in front of her friend. "Leah, this is Jean Lafitte."

He took her hand and kissed it. "Good afternoon, belle gosse."

"Well, don't you have some manners," Leah replied, amused.

"Don't let him charm you," Juliet warned. "He's still a pirate and a thief." She gestured to Leah's ear. "He'll steal those gold earrings right out of your ears if you don't watch yourself."

"I assure you that I shall not," Lafitte interjected. "They are not genuine gold anyway. I would not get much for them. Perhaps half a pence."

With a frown, Leah grabbed her earring with a possessive grip. "My mamere gave them to me." She turned to Juliet. "So, he's stayin' here?"

"Yup, I can't leave him alone again. Who knows what he might do next? Burn down half the city? It's already gone through two great fires..."

"Well, if he's stayin' here, let's put him to work. He could pretend to be a reenactor of himself and entertain the customers. The drunks won't know the difference."

In one swift motion, Jean Lafitte stood from his stool and pushed his cloak behind him. "I can regale your guests with my adventures on the open seas. Tell them how I came face to face with a shark and nearly lost my arm until I fought it off with my sword."

"As long as they buy more drinks, I don't care what you tell them," Leah said. "You'll be our special guest for the Halloween season."

Derek finished serving drinks and joined the threesome at the bar. He nodded toward Jean Lafitte. "I threw you outta here the other night. You're that drunk who thinks he's a pirate."

"He *is* a pirate," Juliet explained and blew out an exasperated sigh. "Long story, but he's who he says he is. Jean Lafitte."

"Pleasure to meet you again, my good man." Jean Lafitte offered his right hand to Derek. "I offer you no ill will regarding our first acquaintance."

Crossing his arms over his burly chest, Derek glanced at Juliet and back again and Jean Lafitte. During his days as a bouncer, he never once even considered meeting an actual pirate. "This guy for real, Jules?"

"Yup," Juliet said. "He needs to stay here with me until I'm done working, otherwise he might make a mess all over The Quarter, in his wake. He already stole a horse and I had to bail him out of jail." A low grumble escaped from her lips.

"Okay, put him to work. But I'm not payin' him. He can keep any tips he makes." Derek stuffed his hands in his pockets.

For the next four hours, Jean Lafitte wandered from table to table introducing himself as an early owner of the ancient building. He stood tall on the wooden tables and recounted tales of the open seas and the treasures he stole. A shot of rum was clenched in his hand.

"Avast ye hearties! Let me tell you a tale that only a seadog like myself could survive. My crew and I sailed through a storm on the Gulf of Mexico that would have sent most landlubbers to Davy Jones' Locker."

Several customers cat-called and applauded.

Lafitte swallowed a mouthful of rum. "But aye, our mission was calling. A mission to Hispaniola to claim a booty that was ours. Nothing would stand in our way, not even the briny deep. We raised the Jolly Roger and claimed victory over the unforgiving seas."

More clientele gathered around him, sliding chairs and tables close by.

He continued, "When we came ashore, we were met with the Spanish army but they were no match for us. I ran a shot across the bow and they retreated. We got our land legs and defeated them in no time. Our bounty awaited us full of gold doubloons and priceless jewels."

Customers laughed, applauded, and listened with intrigue as he raised his sword remembering the adventures he had. No one questioned who he really was.

At the bar, Juliet and Leah kept an eye on him as they poured drinks. "What're you doing with him when you're done working tonight?" Leah asked her.

"Probably working on where to find his cursed jewels. I'm sure he has some ideas after stewing on a ship for two hundred years, but he hasn't told me much. But he owes me seven hundred dollars for bailing him out of jail."

"Y'all wanna come with me to my Mamere Essie's?" Leah's long curly hair bounced over her shoulders as she chatted. "It's Monday. She's making red beans and rice tonight. And I bet she'll have some more ideas. She knows things about this city that many people don't."

"That sounds fun. We'll be there."

Chapter 15

At 7:00 that night, Leah, Juliet, and Jean Lafitte arrived at Leah's grandmother's house in the batture between the levee and wherever the water level happened to be at the Mississippi. The small community of eccentric wooden homes built on 20 feet high stilts defied modern times. Some were handsome, others ramshackle, but all were unique. Most of the houses had uneven siding that was made with salvaged lumber taken from the river. The blare of a towboat's horn sang in the wind and tugboats pushed past in slow motion along the river with block-long barges. The breeze was cool as the sun set in the western sky. Eagles soared, beavers swam past, and the setting sun was framed by the inky geometry of the distant Huey P. Long Bridge. A few of the homes were decorated for Halloween. The frontier-like community was the polar opposite of the rest of modern and classical New Orleans. These people were on the "wrong side" of the levee. They took the phrase "living on the wrong side of the tracks" to a whole other level. Rumors abound that they didn't pay property tax and that their children barely attended school.

Pushing away a low-hanging branch of an unpruned willow tree, Leah led Juliet and Lafitte along the steady wooden plank walkway to her grandmother's cottage. Tree frogs called out in the evening searching for mates. An old woman wearing a flowing dress rode by them on her pink bicycle, waved, and chimed her bike bell at them. Leah waved back at her. "Evenin', Miss Ginny. How's Mr. Macon?"

"God ain't taken him yet," the woman called as she rode away.

Juliet spoke low to Jean Lafitte, "Please don't make a scene. We're her guests."

"Aye, belle gosse. But I know this part of the river. My ship has traveled it. It has not changed at all. A maze of swamps, bogs, river deltas, and marshes protected my crew, and left hundreds of government bounty hunters in frustration, while the gators lurked nearby."

When the trio approached the front door, Leah's grandmother met them. She was a stout woman who wore a purple and orange turban that covered her gray and white speckled hair. The matching flowing duster she wore reached the floor. Wrinkles spattered her face in the right places. Thick, round-framed glasses surrounded her dark eyes. She looked like she could bare-knuckle box an alligator while reciting the Holy Rosary in Cajun French.

Leah bent down and hugged her. "Mamere Essie!"

"Hi, Sugar. Where y'at?" She kissed her granddaughter on the cheek and then swatted her behind. "What'd I teach you 'bout standin' up straight and bein' a proud Black woman?"

Smiling, Leah straightened her shoulders and stood erect. "Yes, ma'am."

"Our Broussard family goes back five generations. Just because we ain't Garden District rich don't mean we can't stand tall."

"Yes, ma'am."

Despite being a head shorter, Essie shouldered past Leah and scrutinized the two other people on her uneven porch. The man in the pirate costume held most of her attention. "Who's your guests, sha?"

"This is my friend Juliet." Leah grabbed Juliet by the arm. "I told you about her. She works with me at the tavern."

The old woman studied Juliet for a moment, then wrapped her arms around Juliet's thin frame. "You look like you need to eat somethin'. I'll fatten you up."

Juliet exchanged glances with Leah as Essie squeezed her tight. "So, happy to meet you."

"Call me Miss Essie." She then put her attention on Jean Lafitte. With squinting dark eyes, she cocked her head to the side and licked her lips a few times. "What're you s'posed to be?"

"I am Jean L-" he started to say and tipped his tricorn hat.

"Jean," Leah interrupted. "His name is Jean. We hired him at the tavern to entertain customers."

"Don't lie to me, Sugar." Her dark eyes bore into her granddaughter. "There's somethin' 'bout him. I can feel it."

"You're right, Mamere," Leah replied. "He's not just an entertainer."

"I am Jean Lafitte the Pirate. The Terror of the Gulf." He bowed to her and took his place next to Juliet again.

Juliet held her breath, anxious to hear what Essie thought of Jean Lafitte.

Essie sniffed upward into his tall frame. She poked a finger at him several times, inspecting his solidity. "You're alive."

"Aye," he replied. "Marie Laveau cursed my crew and me. I have less than a fortnight to retrieve the jewels she stole from me two hundred years ago. I must return them to Isla Mujeres before the moon turns full. I have been told you can assist me."

"I can, but let's eat first." She led the threesome into her vine-covered home and Jean Lafitte removed his hat. "I hope y'all are hungry. I got pots o' gumbo and red beans and rice ready for y'all." They followed her to the compact kitchen, avoiding the cracks in the floorboards. Essie gestured for them to sit at the small metal table as she went to her stove. Steam rose from two large cast iron pots as intoxicating smells of roux, gulf seafood, and the inimitable smokiness of andouille filled the air. With a wooden spoon, she stirred the gumbo counter-clockwise and filled mismatched bowls with the soupy concoction. Every superstitious New Orleanian knew that stirring gumbo counter-clockwise encouraged a quiet hurricane season. As a final touch, she sprinkled some file' seasoning on the gumbo.

"How do you like workin' with my favorite granddaughter?" Essie asked Juliet.

As Leah blushed, Juliet answered, "It's great, Miss Essie. She showed me the ropes and I'm glad we're friends."

"'At's so nice to hear. And where are you from, darlin'?" Essie handed her a steaming bowl.

"Baltimore, born and raised."

"How's ya mama an' them?"

"Oh, I, my--" Juliet lowered her eyes, glanced away quickly, and then back again at Essie. "My parents passed away ten years ago. Right after I graduated college."

"Bless ya heart, sha." Essie lovingly cupped Juliet's cheek. She turned to Jean Lafitte and handed him his bowl of gumbo.

With a quiet exhale, Juliet changed the subject, "Thank you for dinner, Miss Essie. This looks delicious. Had I had more time, I would have made a dessert."

"No worries, sha. Next time." Essie flicked a dismissive hand at her. "The gumbo is an ol' family recipe. The roux is the secret. I stand by the stove and stir that flour and oil patiently until it's a perfect brown with a wooden spoon, because gumbo needs some lovin' with a wooden spoon. Some Yanks think tomatoes go in gumbo. But any cooyon with half a brain knows that tomatoes nevah, evah go in gumbo. Tomatoes are for spaghetti sauce. Ain't that right, Sugar?"

"Yes, ma'am," Leah answered with a grin.

If Juliet ever put gumbo on a future menu, she'd know who to come to for the best advice. The smooth, thick gumbo coated the back of her throat.

"That's another reason why your mama named you Leah." Essie grinned, her mouth full of weathered teeth, and even missing a few. She turned to Juliet. "You know how Leah got her name?"

"No, ma'am."

"Why, we named her after our city's favorite daughter, Leah Chase. The queen of Creole cuisine. She never turned no one away and even fed a few high and mighty presidents. There's a picture of Barack Obama huggin' her hangin' in her restaurant in Tremé."

"Yes, Mamere." Leah blushed.

"Why do we cook red beans and rice on Mondays?" Juliet asked.

Turning back to the stove, the wooden floors creaking beneath her, Essie filled more bowls with the traditional dish. "Monday was typically wash day, and the beans simmered all day on the back of the stove while laundry was done. It's always been like that. An' everyone knows you only use Camellia beans."

Essie served them the red beans and rice and took a seat with them at the small table. She took Leah and Juliet's hands in hers, and the young women grabbed Jean Lafitte's. Essie prayed, "Bless us and this food which we share with grateful hearts. Thank you for putting us together as family and friends. Steer our hearts to Your purpose for our lives. Amen."

"Amen," the young women responded. Jean Lafitte stayed silent.

"Why you quiet?" Essie asked the pirate. "We all go to Mass around here."

"Most pirates forsake religion," he answered.

"Nonsense! Ev'ryone has some kind of faith. I bet you prayed to the Lawd when your ship was in the middle of a hurricane."

"Aye," Lafitte smirked. "You fascinate me. You could join my crew. Teach some of my men a thing or two."

"Some other life, darlin'." Essie gestured to the meal in front of them that she made. "Y'all eat, now."

As they lapped up gumbo and red beans and rice, Jean Lafitte spoke up, "This food is delectable. I prefer it over-salted beef and dried biscuits that I ate every night on my ship. Though the grog made it palatable."

Across the table, Essie pointed her spoon at him. "Now that y'all have eaten some, let's talk 'bout you now."

"I am searching for cursed jewels. Jewels that have kept my crew on *The Pride* for two hundred years. Marie Laveau stole them from me. Apparently, this is how she gained power. We will return the jewels to Isla Mujeres and break the curse. Then, and only then, can we be free."

"Where 'ave you looked so far?" Essie asked.

"This morning, I attempted to go into the French Quarter toward a side street where I had disreputable, yet valuable, contacts, but none of the buildings were what I expected. I will need to search again. I have waited long enough."

"Then he was arrested for peeing in the alley and resisting arrest," Juliet spoke up. "I had to bail him out of jail."

"Aye, belle gosse. I am in your debt." He turned back to Essie. "I have less than a fortnight to recover and return the jewels. Otherwise, my crew and I will be banished to the Mississippi for eternity."

"You've already been to the cemetery to see Marie Laveau's tomb?" Essie pushed her glasses upward on her nose.

"Aye. Nothing substantial came of it."

"We also went on a ghost tour to give him some ideas," Juliet added.

"I have someone you can talk to," Essie said. "Madame Delia. She and I go way back. She keeps her spiritual secrets close like I keep my gumbo recipe." Essie winked at them.

"Madame Delia? Why do I know that name?" Leah wondered.

"She has a gris-gris shop across from Preservation Hall."

"No, that's not it." Leah tapped a couple of fingers against her chin. "Oh, I know. My friend Elle who works at Antoine's told me about her. Elle didn't believe at first, but said she's the real deal. She told me Madame Delia blessed her baby daughter Camille to keep the bad spirits away."

Essie spoke again, "Go see Madame Delia. She's the one to help you."

Chapter 16

The next morning, before work, Juliet and Jean Lafitte trekked to the middle of the French Quarter, to St. Peter Street. A sign for the upcoming annual Zombie Run was fastened to a nearby lamp post. Halloween in New Orleans brought out the misfits more than ever. The vampires would be out. The voodoo queens, too. All sorts of cranks and ne'er-do-wells, tricksters, pranksters, con-men, river sharks, hucksters, street preachers, sheet ghosts, hobgoblins and rougaroux, and zombies, too, they would be out and about. Sane people would stay home to work on their Mardi Gras costumes. October was seductive to almost everyone.

Across the narrow one-way road from Preservation Hall was an unassuming weathered two-story light pink building with green shutters. The lopsided second-story balcony had seen better days.

"When I went to a show here," Juliet said, "we weren't allowed to take pictures during the performance. It's like they have their own secrets to keep."

"Strange." Jean Lafitte twirled his mustache. "Perhaps they know something about the jewels too? Let us go in."

"Not now. They're closed during the day." Juliet pointed to another shop. "*This* is why we're here."

The doorway on the right of Preservation Hall sported a small beige sign that read: `Madame Delia's Spirits`. The sign was so obscure that Juliet wondered if most people even saw it from the street.

"This is it," Juliet said. She swallowed hard and led Lafitte inside.

The interior of the shop had the makings of an old general store protected from a phantom. Colorful beads and gris-gris cluttered the ceiling, forcing tall patrons to duck. Candles touting purity, protection, peace, and love filled small boxes like an old-fashioned mail slot. Voodoo dolls dressed in makeshift clothes intermixed with figurines of the Virgin Mary and crosses. Carved wooden masks hung from a metal rack gawked at them from the corner of the room. A few curious tourists perused the mystical trinkets.

Behind the glass display case full of cigars, the back of a stout woman faced them. She was in the process of adjusting the wall of wooden masks behind the counter.

"It is nice to meet you, Juliet," the woman said without facing them.

"Whoa," Juliet whispered to Lafitte, shocked that the woman knew her name without ever meeting her before. "Madame Delia?"

"Yes, Juliet." The woman turned around to face them. "And you, Jean Lafitte." Gold necklaces overlaid her long, flowy purple dress. A black silk scarf wrapped through her white hair. Matching gold hoop earrings reached her shoulders. Deep lines set in her face sagged beneath soulful silver eyes. A weathered, hand-carved cane rested against the counter. "You are searching for your treasure."

"How--?" he started to say, but Juliet hushed him to let the old woman continue.

As if in a trance, Madame Delia closed her eyes and hummed for a few seconds, then opened them. "Six pieces. Three pairs of two. Emeralds for wit, royalty, and foresight. Rubies for power, wealth, and protection. Sapphires for luck, loyalty, and love."

"Aye," Lafitte replied. "From Isla Mujeres. The women there were powerful because of the stones. My Gunner Cedric stole the jewels and brought them here. Before I could return them, Marie Laveau stole them from me--"

"And gained her power with them," Madame Delia finished his sentence.

"Aye." He nodded slowly. "I have less than a fortnight to find the jewels and return them. Before the moon is full."

Juliet added, "Can you help us find them?" Her confident, fixed gaze lay on the old woman, but unsure of the mystical powers she held.

"Yes," she answered. "Three blocks northeast of here, on St. Philip, The Lady of the Night will have answers for you."

"A prostitute?" Juliet furrowed her brow in confusion.

"No," Madame Delia replied. "She is a spirit at MRB Bar."

"Oh!" Juliet shook her head. "She's the one who seeks out women and steals their jewelry."

"*Beautiful* women," Jean Lafitte added.

"How will we convince her to help us?" Juliet asked.

"If you bring her something to appease her--" Madame Delia gestured toward the shiny trinkets in a nearby display case, "--she may cooperate. I would advise you two to stay together." She turned to Juliet. "Do not go in alone. Even though you can see what he sees."

Juliet gasped and a chill ran up her spine. "Wow. You are the real deal. Leah's friend was right."

Ignoring them, Jean Lafitte grabbed a handful of sparkly rings and bracelets from the display case. "Will these suffice for The Lady of the Night?"

"I would assume so," Madame Delia said.

Lafitte handed them to Madame Delia as Juliet pulled her wallet out. She mentally ran up his tab. He was pushing a thousand dollars. Hopefully, she'd see some returns for her invested assistance. The rake was growing on her even though he was a pain in the ass. Her dream of being a pastry chef again would have to be put on hold. At least for the next two weeks.

* * * *

Ten minutes later, they were at Lafitte's Blacksmith Shop Bar. Juliet served Purple Drank to the clientele next to Leah as Jean Lafitte resumed his role as the in-house entertainer.

"What did Madame Delia have to say, Jules?" Leah wanted to know.

"She told us to go to MRB and talk to the female ghost there."

"Well, while you were gone, I found this." Leah handed her phone to Juliet. A news article was on the screen.

Juliet's nostrils flared as she read it. "What the hell?" She glared at Jean Lafitte who was on the other side of the room recounting tales of the high seas.

She ran across the bar and yanked him away from his adoring fans.

"Belle gosse!" he cried.

"Don't belle gosse me!" she spat. "Who the hell are you?"

"I am Captain Jean Lafitte." He swept his red cloak behind him, removed his tricorn hat, and bowed to her. "I have been haunting the Mississippi for the past two hundred years."

She shoved Leah's phone in his face. "Not according to this. Are you scamming me?"

147

He read the headline out loud, "Pirate Jean Laffite faked his death and moved to Lincolnton..." He frowned and tilted his head to the side. "Where is Lincolnton?"

"North Carolina," Juliet hissed. "But that's not the point. The point is that it says the real Jean Lafitte disappeared in the Caribbean and then resurfaced in North Carolina with a new name to hide from his enemies. Not that he's been haunting the Mississippi because of cursed jewels."

"Putain! Whoever wrote this deserves a cleave-him-to-the -brisket!"

Juliet shook her head in confusion and grabbed Leah's phone out of his hand. "I don't know what that means, but you need to tell me the truth. Who *are* you? Or I swear to God I'll take you back to the police station and let you rot in jail for the next 10 days." She clenched a fist. "There's no treasure, is there?"

"I am indeed Jean Lafitte." As he thrust his chest out, he lifted his heels and stood upright as he emphasized his words. "I have been waiting on *The Pride* long enough! Whoever that scallywag is in North Carolina t'was not me. If I find my impersonator, the scurvy dog shall walk the plank." His lips flattened into a thin line.

"You expect me to believe you?" Juliet hissed. "Just because you say so?" The costumed customers around them quieted and gawked at their argument.

Juliet heard one say to his friend, "This guy's really getting into character."

"Aye, I am him. I swear on my brother Pierre's life." Lafitte settled back against the brick fireplace in the center of the room with an exaggerated casualness.

"Not. Good. Enough," Juliet scowled through gritted teeth. His arrogance and nonchalance infuriated her.

"You have seen for yourself the spirits we have encountered when you are with me," he said. "It is not witchcraft. I am not running a rig with you."

Juliet blew out an exasperated sigh. He was right. Even though the city was full of haunting tales, she had never seen one until she touched Jean Lafitte. Despite all of the ghostly legends she had heard about in her adopted city, she always held the stories at arm's length, not knowing if they were true. Until now.

"Please," he begged. "I swear I am him. I need you to assist me to retrieve the cursed jewels. Despite what I stated earlier, I do trust you."

"What about the bail money I spent?" Juliet cocked an eyebrow at him. She wasn't convinced. "How are you paying me back for that?"

"I promise you on the soul of my brother that I shall reimburse you." He held his right hand out to her.

Juliet looked at him, glanced aside toward Leah at the bar, and back at Jean Lafitte. She shook his hand and, at that moment, Juliet saw a black specter floating through the wooden rafters above them. "Holy smokes," she muttered, watching the apparition waft above them.

"Leah, you seeing this?" Juliet couldn't take her eyes off the phantom as she gripped Jean Lafitte's hand.

Leah called from the bar and gazed upward, "See what?"

Pointing upward, Juliet's mouth fell into an O. "That."

Nearby customers looked up to where Juliet motioned, but saw nothing as well.

"I did not hornswoggle you." Lafitte released Juliet's hand and she no longer saw the ghostly spirit above her.

How did this happen to her? Last week she was serving Purple Drank to inebriated tourists while hoping for a new pastry job. Now she could watch the departed souls of the city who never left. She wasn't sure if she liked this newfound skill. Jean Lafitte's shared power allowing her to visualize all this gained her respect. He was slowly growing on her.

"Shall we go see The Lady of the Night tonight?" Jean Lafitte asked her.

Chapter 17

After Juliet finished working that night, she and Jean Lafitte made their way to MRB Bar three blocks away. Halloween revelers wandered in and out of the open green wooden doors as rock music blared from inside. A wooden A-frame sign perched on the sidewalk at the entrance boasting a hundred types of beers, frozen drinks, and oysters.

Outside the two-story tan building, Juliet smiled that she left her mother's bracelet at home. The invaluable piece of jewelry would not be plucked by the resident ghostly kleptomaniac.

Inside, the bartender gestured to Jean Lafitte's pirate attire. "Hey Jack Sparrow, what can I get you? A Green Drank?"

Lafitte talked to Juliet out of the side of his mouth, "I am growing tired of being called that. What a landlubber."

The bartender said, "I've seen a few pirates like you wandering the streets lately. More than usual."

Lafitte ignored his comment and slapped a hand on the glossy bar. "I shall have some rum!"

"Comin' up. What kind of rum?"

"Grog."

"Grog?" The bartender arched an eyebrow in confusion.

Juliet skirted around Jean Lafitte and spoke to the bartender, "He means Bacardi. On the rocks. Make it two." She pulled her credit card out and handed it to the barkeep. "I'm buying."

"You got it."

While Juliet and Jean Lafitte waited for their drinks, they studied the room. A handful of patrons played pool in the back corner. At the tables, customers noshed on platters of shucked oysters. Staff hurried around serving drinks and food. The place was lively but not packed full of patrons.

"Do you see her?" Juliet asked.

"No. She may be in the courtyard."

"Or the ladies' room." Juliet swallowed hard, remembering what their ghost tour guide warned about the resident ghost. Using her fingertips, she made sure the rings and bracelets from Madame Delia were in her jeans pocket.

The bartender interrupted them by placing two highball glasses full of rum on the bar next to them. Juliet sipped her drink while Lafitte threw his back in one gulp. "Another!" He thumped the empty glass on the bar.

"Don't get drunk on me," Juliet warned, tapping his forearm. "I can't talk to the ghosts without you."

"Aye." He smiled wide underneath his mustache. "You are a fine belle gosse. You would fit in with my crew. You make me proud."

Suddenly, a shriek came from the restroom and a frantic woman emerged. Tears streamed down her cheeks and she held her fingers to a new bruise on her forehead. "SHE attacked me!" The bartender rushed to the woman's side as other concerned customers assisted the woman. They sat her on a nearby chair. "I was in the restroom washin' my hands and this ghostly woman in white appeared behind me in the mirror. Next thing I know, she slammed my head against the sink and stole my necklace." She ran a few fingers along her bare collarbone.

"You're not bleedin'," the bartender consoled her as he dabbed a napkin to her face. "But you have a nice goose egg on your forehead."

"Guess we know where she is," Juliet said to Lafitte.

He stood quickly from his stool and rushed toward the restroom. Juliet was on his heels. As he reached for the door, she stopped him. "Wait. You can't go in there."

"Why not?" A blank look formed on his face.

"Because it's the *ladies' room*," Juliet answered. "You're not a lady."

"Then you must go in," Lafitte instructed. "Weigh anchor and hoist the mizzen."

"Huh?" Juliet cocked her head to the side.

"Move in and draw her out. Offer your jewels. This is the first real clue to finding the cursed booty."

"Aye, aye, Captain." Juliet mock saluted him, swallowed hard, and pushed the door open.

As her shoulders tightened, Juliet tiptoed around the empty restroom. "Hello-o? Lady of the Night? Are you here?"

One of the faucets turned on and Juliet jumped back, catching her breath. "Holy shit," she muttered under her breath. She reached inside her pocket and slowly pulled out the rings from Madame Delia. She kept the bracelets hidden as a future bargaining chip. "Here, I have something for you. These are for you if you can help my friend and me." With her eyes clenched shut, Juliet raised her palm full of shiny bling and waited for The Lady of the Night to make her move. When nothing immediately happened, Juliet popped one eye open, and then the other.

Jean Lafitte called through a crack in the door, "Shall I come in?"

"Yeah," Juliet sighed, still holding her hand up. "I don't see her."

Creaking the old wooden door open, Lafitte stepped inside the restroom and moved toward the opposite wall. "Good evening, m'lady." He removed his tricorne hat and bowed to the empty corner. Juliet held her breath and watched him. He spoke again, "I do not often make deals with those I do not trust, but I must make an exception. Do you see the jewels the belle gosse is holding?" He motioned for Juliet to come closer to him. "They shall be yours if you assist us."

Lafitte grabbed Juliet's free hand and The Lady of the Night appeared before her. A chill filled the room. "Wow," Juliet gasped. If she had a free hand, she would have pulled her phone out and snapped a picture. No one would believe her otherwise.

Dressed in a long, white gown, the semi-transparent mystical woman nodded, never taking her vacant eyes off of Juliet's rings. Her hair, once golden, now hung in disheveled strands, and her hands were bony and skeletal, forever reaching out in search of sparkly trinkets. Adorned in a flowing gown, the fabric was a delicate, faded hue, once vibrant but now touched by the passage of years. Layers of sheer chiffon cascaded gracefully, creating an otherworldly silhouette that floated in the air. The gown's neckline was low, evoking a sense of immodesty characteristic of the 1800s prostitutes, with intricate lace detailing that spoke to a bygone era's intricate craftsmanship.

Lafitte spoke again, "I am in search of six jewels. Two emeralds, two sapphires, and two rubies. It is of utmost importance that I find them. Are you aware of any of them?"

"No," The Lady of the Night breathed out. Her voice was low and husky. "Go away."

Jean Lafitte didn't like to lose the upper hand. He was known as the Terror of the Gulf for a reason. The Lady of the Night was lying. Deep down in his gut, he knew it. His hunches were always right. He slowly nodded to Juliet.

Picking up on his silent direction, Juliet cupped the rings in her hand and reached into her pocket for the bracelets. "You can have all of these if you help us."

Intrigued by the additional sparkles, The Lady of the Night hovered closer to them. "Hmmm." When she attempted to grab the jewels out of Juliet's hand, Lafitte quickly clamped his hand over Juliet's.

"Not yet," he said. A wry smile formed under his mustache. "They are all yours if you supply us with information first."

"I have had the emeralds for a hundred years," The Lady of the Night spoke. "But you cannot have them. They are worth more than those trinkets you offer. Come back when you have something else that is worthy of my time." With that, she disappeared into the wall.

With a frustrated huff, Juliet shoved the rings and bracelets back into her pocket. "That was a bust. We didn't even get a chance to ask her how she got the emeralds from Marie Laveau."

"I disagree." Lafitte shook his head. "She gave us a bounty of information. We shall come back when we have something of more value to trade. I am not defeated."

Before Juliet could respond, a woman entered the bathroom, caught sight of Jean Lafitte, and high-tailed it out of there. "I'll hold it," she muttered on the way out.

"You still have a way with women," Juliet joked. "The wrong way, but still a way."

Chapter 18

The next morning, Jean Lafitte found Juliet in her kitchen still wearing pajamas and sipping a cup of coffee.

"Want some?" she offered, pushing a strand of her blonde hair behind her ear. "It's hot and strong."

"Not this morning." He climbed on the stool next to her at the island. He wore the sweats that she had bought him a few days earlier, after realizing they were comfy to sleep in. Sans tricorn hat, his thick black hair wisped into small waves.

"You hungry?"

"Aye. Calas would be lovely. My brother and I dined on them many mornings together. Are you familiar?"

"Of course." Juliet's face sparkled, happy to make a favorite New Orleans treat. "They're still a thing around here. They're easier and faster to make than the beignets we had." Leaving her coffee mug on the counter, she grabbed a mixing bowl from her cabinet. Then she headed to her pantry and pulled out flour, sugar, baking powder, salt, vanilla, confectioners' sugar, and oil. From the fridge, she grabbed two eggs and some leftover cooked rice. Being a pastry chef, her kitchen was always stocked with these items.

"May I assist you?"

"No, I got this." She stirred the dry ingredients and mixed in the rice until it was thoroughly coated. The cold rice prevented the batter from clumping together. "Did you and Pierre make calas?"

"No. Slaves and free people of color who brought the cakes from Africa via the slave trade sold them in the streets. They would call, 'Calas, calas! *Belle calas tout chaud.*'"

"What does that mean?" Juliet stopped mid-stirring and gaped at him.

"Nice warm calas." He winked at her.

Despite their rocky start, the past few days had been a welcome adventure for Juliet. If it wasn't for Jean Lafitte, she would have been shaking martinis all week. Sure, she had a great time working with Leah and Derek, but the occasional late nights were killer. She was used to getting up early to whip up milk and cookies at Willa Jean. The Valrhona chocolate and delicate crystals of fleur de sel concoctions were morning favorites among all-night partiers from Bourbon Street. Now her new sleep schedule was enough to make her start seeing things. Oh wait, she was. This new ability to see ghosts freaked her out sometimes. The Lady of the Night came close enough and Juliet escaped without a scratch -- unlike that woman in the bathroom at MRB.

Juliet heated the oil for the calas in a frying pan as Jean Lafitte watched her. When the oil was hot enough, she dropped the rice mixture in and fried them. Within a few minutes, the crispy, plump fritters begged to be served with obscene quantities of confectioners' sugar. Juliet dusted them, turning them from golden brown to covered in white sweetness in a matter of seconds.

"Here you go." Juliet presented a plateful to Jean Lafitte.

He took a bite and puffed confectioner's sugar all over the counter.

"You're cleaning that up," Juliet laughed. "I'm not the maid."

"You are deserving of one." Lafitte popped the rest of the calas into his mouth.

"Can't afford one." Juliet munched on a fritter.

"Once we retrieve the jewels, you shall."

"Speaking of that, where are we going tonight? You gotta come with me to work again today, but after that, I'm free."

Before Lafitte could answer, Juliet's phone rang.

She glanced at the caller ID. "It's Leah. Let me take this."

"Hey Jules," Leah said, "I was supposed to meet my auntie and uncle at Muriel's tonight, but they bailed on me. I have a reservation for three if y'all want to join me. I hate to lose the reservation. It's so hard to get into that place."

Juliet glanced over at Jean Lafitte noshing on more calas. She answered Leah for the both of them, "Yeah, we'd love to. I have to work until 6:00 though."

"Me too," Leah said. "The reservation's for 8:00. We'll be fine."

"Great. See you in a few."

In thirty minutes, Jean Lafitte was back in his red velvet cloak and breeches. His sword was at his side. Juliet slipped on purple Chuck Taylors and a Red Hot Chili Peppers T-shirt and holey jeans. She grabbed some of the leftover calas in a bag and they headed out the door.

A half mile later, they stopped near the entrance of Lafitte's Blacksmith Shop Bar. A saxophonist perched on top of a metal folding chair on the sidewalk by the bar. He puffed out a soulful melody of "Do You Know What It Means To Miss New Orleans?"

"Morning, Abraham." Juliet reached inside her bag and handed the aging street musician a calas as Lafitte stepped toward the bar. "Haven't seen you around in a while."

He stopped playing and lowered his shiny, gold instrument. "Where y'at, Miss Juliet? I know. It's been a few weeks. Doctor said I had a bad ticker and thinks it's time for me to hang up my horn. I tell him 'Ain't no way, Doc, 'cause tootin' this horn is my life.' So, he says to take it easy for a few weeks. I been on this corner for twenty years and I'll be here another twenty, the good Lord willin'." Abraham bit into the calas, dropping a few crumbs on his long white beard. "This here's the best tastin' calas I ever had. You're a darlin' angel." He tipped his saxophone in gratitude toward Juliet.

"Thanks, Abraham. I gotta get to work. Play well today." She smiled and allowed Lafitte to open the door to the bar for her.

In the bar, Juliet found Leah flipping wooden chairs from tabletops to the floor prepping for opening. As Juliet grabbed a chair, she motioned to the pirate. "Hey Lafitte, help us out."

"I am the captain," he balked, "not a powder monkey." He stood rigid near the brick fireplace in the middle of the room.

"You'll help us or I'm kicking you out of my house," Juliet shot back. "And you're on your own to find your jewels." She glared him down, silently daring him to challenge her.

He lost the ultimatum and lowered his shoulders in defeat. "Very well." He indignantly thrust his nose into the air and clomped over to the back room to assemble chairs near the piano.

When Juliet was finished with hers, she walked over to help him. As she stepped closer, she stopped in her tracks and gasped.

"What is it, belle gosse?" Lafitte halted moving chairs and gaped at her.

"The phantom red eyes... in the corner..." Juliet gulped and pointed. A chill ran up her spine. "They were...staring at me."

When Lafitte looked fixedly where she motioned, he shook his head. "I see nothing."

"Really? You see everything."

"Not this occurrence. Perhaps next time."

"I don't want there to be a next time. These things creep me out."

* * * *

After a few hours of hustling drinks and cleaning tables, Juliet finally took a quick break and downed a glass of water. The number of customers exploded throughout the early afternoon. Jean Lafitte entertained the clientele with his tales in the back room.

"You okay?" Leah joined her in the corner.

"Yep, just taking a breather. We're three deep and it's only gonna get worse later. When's Derek coming?"

Leah glanced at her watch; it partially covered a tattoo of a pink rose and the words 'La Vie' written in calligraphy. "Three more hours."

"Let's do this." Juliet headed behind the bar and Leah took off toward tables full of customers.

A group of guys approached Juliet as she laid bev naps in front of them. "What can I get you?"

The one in front motioned to the draft taps beside them. "A pitcher of Abita."

"Coming up." Juliet filled a pitcher and offered a professional smile.

The mid-twenties guy pointed to a large etching of unidentifiable letters on the cement wall behind Juliet's head. "What's that say?" His buddies left him to find a table.

"Nobody knows," Juliet replied. She half-watched him and half-watched the pitcher so it wouldn't overflow. "We tried to wash it off and it reappeared."

"Sounds like the resident ghost is makin' himself known." He looped the bundle of plastic Mardi Gras beads around his neck through his fingers.

"Maybe," Juliet smirked and finished filling the pitcher then grabbed four plastic cups.

"Don't worry. I'll protect you."

"I'm good, thanks." She pushed the pitcher and cups toward him. "That'll be sixteen dollars."

The guy laid down a twenty and leaned over the edge of the bar toward Juliet. His multi-colored beads hung low. "Keep the change. There's more where that came from if you wanna earn it. What do you wanna do for these beads?" He closed his hand into a loose fist and motioned it toward his mouth as if he was swallowing it.

"Ew," Juliet muttered. She slammed the pitcher onto the bar and wanted to gag. Who did he think she was? A drunk tourist? She had been hit on before, but never propositioned like this. And not once as a pastry chef. She couldn't wait to be one again. "No, thanks."

"Oh, come on, you're a dime," he countered. "Girls like you give it up all the time."

"The belle gosse said no," Jean Lafitte said from behind the guy.

The creep's eyes flitted and he flung around, coming face to face with the pirate. Anger pulsed out of his nostrils and he snarled, "Who the hell are you? Jack Sparrow?"

Lafitte scoffed at the tired nickname. "Leave her be."

The jerk set his shoulders and spittle came out of his mouth. He sneered, "Get outta my business, asshole."

In an instant, he laid down the pitcher and took a swing at Lafitte. The pirate deftly ducked, pulled his cutlass from his sash, and jabbed it within inches of the man's face. Lafitte's long hair fluttered slightly in his anticipation. "I told you the belle gosse said no." The whole bar fell silent. Juliet froze in place, waiting for the next move.

The guy saw all of the eyes on him and stepped back. "You ain't worth it." He and his buddies headed out the door, leaving their fresh pitcher of beer behind.

"Wow," Juliet breathed out and said to Jean Lafitte. Not only did she not have to deal with the creep, the machismo pirate lost his chauvinistic attitude and came to her rescue. "Thank you. What a jerk."

"My pleasure." He inserted his sword back into his sash and tipped his chin at her. "T'was not the first time I was unexpectedly crossed."

"How so?"

"One night, I dined with a fair maiden not far from here and was challenged three separate times. I offered my enemies the chance to leave with their lives and dignities intact, but they refused. I apologized to my female companion and drew my rapier."

"Then what happened?" Juliet wanted to know.

"Three dead men later, I returned unharmed and unflustered to my guest. My filet mignon with cabernet sauce was excellent."

"That's not quite what happened here," Juliet said. "I could've taken care of myself."

"Perhaps, but I was happy to assist." Lafitte wrinkled his nose. "Though he referred to you as a dime. What does that mean?"

Reaching into the tip jar, Juliet pulled out a coin. "This is a dime. It's ten cents. Jerky guys like him rank women from one to ten and he meant I'm a ten, that I'm the best."

Lafitte studied the foreign money, squinting. "So, you're a doubloon?"

"Yeah," Juliet chuckled at the new moniker. "You could say that."

"As I have told you before, you are a fine belle gosse."

"And you're a gentleman."

He winked at her.

Chapter 19

After work, Juliet and Jean Lafitte returned to her house to freshen up before dinner at Muriel's. She changed into a blue short form-fitting dress and ankle boots and Lafitte stayed in his pirate attire.

"It's a fifteen-minute walk, but I'd rather not in these shoes," Juliet said in her front room. "I'll call us a Lyft."

"A lift? Something that raises us?"

"Oh, right." Juliet chuckled. She forgot he was still unfamiliar with many modern inventions. "It's a car service that comes and picks you up."

"Like a horse and carriage?"

"Yes, but without the horse." She punched the Lyft request into her phone. "It'll be here in ten minutes. We'll get to the restaurant right on time."

The dining scene in New Orleans was a food paradise. Diners could satiate their palates with the top-secret recipe of Oysters Rockefeller at Antoine's in the French Quarter, spicy and tangy Barbeque Shrimp at Pascal's Manale in Uptown, and Crawfish Etouffee at Dooky Chase in Tremé.

Fifteen minutes later, the twosome arrived at Muriel's. The massive two-story red brick building lit up the entire corner of St. Ann and Chartres Streets. Black and orange decorations adorned the second-story gallery. Tall, black street lamps illuminated the area. Across the slate courtyard, the Pontalba buildings stretched along the edge of Jackson Square. Its 1840 Parisian-style row house design featured second and third-story intricate iron galleries. Opposite of Muriel's, a dozen people gathered around a vampire-clad tour guide waiting to hear the background of the historic park.

Juliet and Jean Lafitte stepped inside the restaurant's black double doors and met Leah in the vestibule. Her work clothes discarded, Leah wore a brown and yellow flowery dress with flat leather sandals. Layers of thin necklaces hung from her neck. Her mane of curls fell down her back and a few bits of glitter fell to the floor. She stood straight, as her Mamere Essie had taught her.

"Hey, y'all." Leah embraced them. She led them to the host podium and checked in.

The black-suited maître d' guided them into The Bistro. The soul of the restaurant, the dining room reflected family and traditional Southern dining. Finely-dressed couples dined on pecan-crusted drum and the Southern favorite shrimp and grits.

Juliet, Leah, and Jean Lafitte were escorted to a table next to aged brick walls that stretch high to the ceiling. Menus were laid in front of them. Lafitte stood while the women took their seats. Juliet subtly pointed to Lafitte's tricorn hat. He followed her lead and removed it.

"We stopped outside this restaurant on our ghost tour the other night," Juliet said, as a server assistant filled their water glasses.

"Aye," Jean Lafitte added. "The spirit of Monsieur Pierre Antoine Lepardi Jourdan frequents this establishment." He glanced around the crowded dining room. "I do not see him. Yet."

"He was a haughty Frenchman." Leah rolled her eyes. She turned to Lafitte. "Did you hang around them?"

"Occasionally, but they bored me and I found them pretentious," Lafitte said. "I preferred the company of those who led more interesting lives."

"Prostitutes, pirates, and other unquestionable characters?" Juliet cocked an eyebrow as they perused their menus.

"Aye. And I shared my bounty with them if I found them worthy."

"Who did you consider worthy?" Leah asked.

"The poor residents of New Orleans," he replied. "I provided much-needed supplies and foodstuffs to them at low prices, without expectation of real compensation. I often gave the goods away for free."

"Maybe you're not such a badass after all?" Juliet joked.

"I am the King of the Pirates," he puffed out and sat up straight. His cutlass clanged against the chair. "Though I have been known to be chivalrous and kind."

"Kind? Really?" Juliet gaped at him. "Without slicing someone from head to toe with your sword?"

"Aye." Lafitte nodded. "One night, my men and I were playing cards in my den with Vincenzo Gambi and his crew. An argument broke out and Gambi's First Mate accused mine of cheating. I declared, 'We shall have a third party cut the cards.' I sent my blacksmith Thiac to summon one of the fishermen from the coast to my house. When the fisherman arrived, he was nervous with sweat. He had brought his little daughter with him in hopes that we wouldn't kill him in front of his child."

Leah gasped.

"I smiled when I saw the young girl and gently asked her to cut the deck, explaining to her what it meant. She did and I won the hand. Gambi stormed out. I called the girl to my lap, thanked her for her help, and dropped a twenty-dollar gold piece into her palm."

"That girl saw a glimpse of your generosity," Juliet said in more of a statement than a question. "Seems like an exception to your pillaging lifestyle."

"Perhaps." A coy smile formed under Lafitte's mustache. "I have been known to have a temper the length of a cannonball fuse. A group of seamen assembled outside of my home, threatening mutiny. I went outside with a smile, casually shot the leader in the face, and returned to my evening meal without a word."

Shocked, Leah raised a hand to her mouth.

"Don't worry," Juliet noted, "The NOPD confiscated his gun when he was arrested earlier."

"But I still have my sword. I have never lost a duel and was one of the most skilled rapier-duelists of my time."

"If you use it," Juliet warned, a V forming in between her furrowed brows. "I'll call the cops myself and have you thrown in jail and you can forget about finding the jewels."

"Checkmate, belle gosse." He smirked.

A server in a black jacket and matching pants approached them. He smiled at them. "Good evening, my name is Francis and I'll be waiting on you tonight. What drinks can I bring for you? They are the finest hand-crafted cocktails this side of the Mississippi River."

Leah spoke first, "I'll take a Saint 75."

"Excellent choice," Francis said. He turned to Juliet. "And you, miss?"

"A Fleur De Lis."

"Another excellent choice." He nodded toward Jean Lafitte. "And you, sir?"

Lafitte studied the wine and cocktail list and frowned. "Where is your rum? I do not see it."

"Our bar has plenty of rum options," Francis offered. "But might I suggest a Louisiana Rum Runner? We use Don-Q Cristal rum, strawberry-honey puree, banana liqueur, and orange juice."

"How long has the rum aged?" Lafitte leaned forward as if he was testing the waiter.

"One-and-a-half to five years in American white oak barrels in Puerto Rico to impart a touch more smoothness for a cleaner, more refined, and more delicate flavor," Francis volleyed back.

"Puerto Rico! I have been there and I approve."

"Very well," Francis said. "I'll be back shortly with your drinks."

After Francis left, Leah asked Lafitte, "Were you a rum runner in Puerto Rico?"

"Rum runners only smuggled rum," he answered. "I expanded my enterprise to gold, silver, soap, cloth, dyes, spices, and cocoa. My most gainful import was something that is now outlawed." He glanced toward Leah. Her bronze skin glistened under the overhead chandeliers. "It was all quite lucrative."

"How much were you worth?" Juliet wanted to know.

"Millions." He winked at the women.

Francis returned with their drinks. "Have you decided on your dinner selections?"

"Yes," Juliet spoke for all of them. She ordered shrimp and grits, Leah chose the pork chop, and Jean Lafitte wanted the roasted chicken.

After they finished eating, Jean Lafitte grabbed all of the silverware from the table and clutched them against himself.

"Are you stealing the silverware?" Juliet admonished him in an angry murmur.

"Aye. I shall receive a million doubloons for them." He laughed heartily as if Juliet was missing the joke.

"Put them down!" Juliet whispered through gritted teeth. "You're gonna get us kicked out of here before we even get a chance to talk to the ghost upstairs."

Lafitte huffed and placed the silverware back on the table. "Very well."

Soon, Francis brought them a second round of drinks. Juliet asked him, "Are there any private events tonight?"

"No," he said. "You may bring your cocktails into the Séance Lounge upstairs if you would like."

"Yes, we would. Thank you."

Once Francis left again, Juliet leaned closer to her friends. "I figured we could go upstairs and see if we can find the ghost of Pierre Jourdan. Maybe ask him if he knows anything about the cursed jewels."

Chapter 20

The Séance Lounge consisted of two rooms. The outer lounge marked the Storyville era of New Orleans when the surrounding Jackson Square area was part of the French Quarter's best bordellos. Jewel tone décor and plush chaises invited each guest to embrace desires of raw passion. Low lighting set the scene. The inner lounge was sectioned off by a pair of thick maroon velvet drapes that cinched at the wall.

"Monsieur Jourdan?" Juliet called as she led Leah and Lafitte around the empty room. "Are you here? We'd like to ask you a few questions."

A nearby lamp dimmed then relit.

"He's here," Juliet whispered.

Jean Lafitte stepped away from the women; his boots clapping against the wood floor. He ran his hand along the 19th Century furniture scattered throughout the room.

"What are you lookin' for?" Leah asked him.

"Hidden compartments," he said, not looking up at her. "Credenzas and tables like this were used to smuggle priceless items so that the port inspectors could not confiscate them."

"Remove your filthy hands from my desk!" A bodiless voice bellowed around them.

"Show yourself and I shall." Lafitte's hand remained on the antique furniture.

The women froze in place and waited to see what was about to happen.

"I do not take orders from a grungy pirate," the voice commanded.

"Very well." Lafitte put a second hand on the desk, daring the haughty Frenchman to make a move.

Noticing the impasse, Juliet stepped into the middle of the room, her hands open as if she had nothing to hide. "Monsieur Jourdan, I must apologize for my friend." She narrowed her eyes at Lafitte who scoffed in response. "We mean you no harm. We'd like to ask you about some jewels that were stolen two hundred years ago."

"I know nothing about cursed sapphires," Jourdan replied.

Juliet smiled and shared a knowing glance with her friends. "I never said they were cursed or that they were sapphires." She grabbed Leah's hand and placed her other one on Lafitte's shoulder.

"Ah, you have bested me," Jourdan said, his voice filling the room.

Before Juliet could respond, a glimmer of sparkly light lit the inner lounge. Moments later, the figure of a man dressed in a tuxedo appeared before them. The furniture behind him could be seen through his transparent image.

"Oh my god," Leah gasped.

Lafitte removed his hands from the desk and took a step toward Jourdan. Before he took a second step, Juliet motioned for him to stand down. She couldn't risk Lafitte making a threat and losing the opportunity to find answers.

"Monsieur Jourdan, what can you tell us about the sapphires? Are they here?" Juliet asked.

"I have resided in this establishment for over two centuries. The patrons come to see me. This is my home and my livelihood. They adore me here. They set up wine and bread for me every night because they want me. One unfortunate night of gambling has kept me here for eternity." He nodded toward Jean Lafitte. "And I know who you are. I will not be handing my jewels over to a villainous pirate." He stood rigid in front of them.

"They are mine!" Lafitte lurched forward.

Without breaking contact, Juliet and Leah jumped in front of him before he reached Jourdan. They held him back and hushed him.

"My apologies again, Monsieur Jourdan," Juliet said, she turned to face him while simultaneously holding back Lafitte. "How did you come to acquire them? Marie Laveau stole them from Captain Jean Lafitte. We believe that's how she got her power around the city."

Leah added, "She lived until the late 1880s. Well after you committed suicide here."

Jourdan snickered, "Yes, that's true. She did live a long time after me, but..." He rubbed his hand along his chin. "She came to my elegant home for a dinner party and entertained my guests. I saw them in one of her satchels and swiped them from her. I realized I could use my jewels in a future poker game."

"You are forthcoming--" Lafitte began.

"Yes, my apologies." Pierre Jourdan shook his head when he realized his mistake. "I do not usually have visitors who I can converse with."

"And I remember you. You are a lecherous pirate."

"Aye." Lafitte winked at him.

Interrupting them, Juliet glanced around the room. "We understand they are your jewels. But would you be willing to barter for them? Is there something that you value more? A gaming table?"

"Surely, you jest," Jourdan chuckled. "A gaming table is pennies compared to the sapphires. Try again, mademoiselle."

"How about the company of a woman?" Lafitte interrupted. The women loosened their grip on him. Juliet glared at him with daggers for eyes. She knew they couldn't deliver something like that. But she stayed silent.

"Go on." Jourdan's shoulders lowered.

"You must be lonely here," Lafitte began. "Two hundred years without a woman must be torture. I am sure you have manly needs." He stepped away from Leah and Juliet and strode around the room, twirling his mustache between his fingers. "How could you possibly survive?"

"I must admit I am lonely at times." Jourdan lowered his eyes. "My beloved wife has already passed to the other realm. I am here. Alone. I have not passed to the other realm yet. In the meantime, I will enjoy my time and take advantage of the restaurant's hospitality."

"I know of a belle gosse for you," Lafitte said. "She is known as The Lady of the Night. A perfect name."

"She haunts MRB, correct?"

"Aye."

"I have heard she dislikes me," Pierre Jourdan explained. "We ghosts in the city know each other, at least by reputation."

"Nonsense," Lafitte countered. "She told me herself she has admired you for many years now. She only wanted you to believe that she disliked you for her to appear independent and intelligent."

Juliet cringed at the lie.

Lafitte stepped toward Jourdan and offered his hand. "We have an agreement then?"

"Yes." Jourdan shook his hand.

"Where can we find the sapphires?"

"In a remote marble box inside a corner of an antique shop on Rue Royal."

"Why are they no longer in your possession?" Lafitte arched an eyebrow.

"Before I took my own life, after that fateful poker game," Jourdan explained, "I bet the jewels to the antique shop owner."

"Which one?" Juliet finally spoke. Royal Street was known for its different fine antique shops. "And what do you mean by 'remote?'"

"That, mademoiselle, is for you to determine," Jourdan replied. "I shall tell you the answer when I meet The Lady of the Night."

Chapter 21

"Why would you offer up The Lady of the Night?" Juliet shrieked at Jean Lafitte on the sidewalk outside of Muriel's. Inky blue and purple streaks filled the night sky as opulent St. Louis Cathedral dominated the backdrop. Posters for the upcoming Boo of Krewe Halloween Parade were plastered to nearby lamp posts. "We can't give her to Jourdan."

"He does not know that," Lafitte answered. He stepped on the slate Chartres Street Plaza toward the empty metal benches, his heels echoing into the almost-empty area. "We have the advantage. If an enemy does not want money, the fairer sex may be a good substitute."

"I wasn't there when you met The Lady of the Night," Leah added, "but do y'all think she'll agree to it?"

"Hell no," Juliet scoffed. "She attacked some poor woman in MRB and hissed at us when we asked her about the emeralds."

"Again," Lafitte said, "Jourdan does not know that. If I have learned anything in my years as a buccaneer--"

"--that you lie, cheat, and steal?" Juliet finished his sentence.

"Touché, belle gosse." He gripped the back of one of the benches, propped one of his legs on it, and stared into the open space as if he was commandeering *The Pride*. "I have learned that I need to make my enemy believe something that may not be true to get what I want."

"Like I said, lie, cheat, and steal." Juliet rolled her eyes and shook her head. "But what about the other thing that Jourdan told us? That the sapphires are in a marble box in an antique shop on Royal Street."

"There are twenty shops on Royal!" Leah gasped.

"We'll have to go in each one and look for the marble box that he was talking about." Juliet shuffled her feet, unsure where to start.

Lafitte gazed at the moon, the waxing crescent cast a haunting spectacle into the French Quarter. "We have ten days to find the jewels. We cannot waste time."

"Then let's go back to MRB and try to convince The Lady of the Night to meet Jourdan."

Five minutes later, the trio entered the haunted bar. Juliet and Leah headed into the ladies' room, but returned seconds later.

"We need your help to see her," Juliet said to Jean Lafitte.

"Very well." He entered the restroom with Juliet while Leah kept watch for unsuspecting clientele to block them from coming in.

As Lafitte bowed, The Lady of the Night came into view. "Good evening, m'lady."

"What of value did you bring to me?" she spoke, tapping her long fingers with calculation on a nearby sink.

"The company of a Frenchman," Lafitte answered. "Surely, you must be lonely here."

"You must take me for a fool!" she hissed. "I am no longer a trollop. Get out! Get out!" The mirrors in the bathroom cracked into glass webs as she bellowed.

Leaving Lafitte to fend for himself, Juliet bolted out of the bathroom, through the bar area, and onto the sidewalk. Leah was two steps behind.

"Jules! What happened in there?" Leah asked, catching her breath.

"The Lady of the Night is no longer a lady of the night," Juliet said. She turned to Lafitte, who had caught up with them, but didn't seem to be out of breath. "What do we do now?"

"We must find the sapphires that Jourdan spoke of." He twirled his mustache between his fingers. "And make haste."

Chapter 22

For the next three days, Juliet, Jean Lafitte, and sometimes Derek and Leah, scoured antique shops along Royal Street, one of the oldest streets in the city. The historic street had a long-standing reputation for being the spot to track down rare and much sought-after items. The group went before work, during lunch breaks, and after work, before the shops closed. They hit Antiques De Provence, M.S. Rau Antiques, Sigle's Antiques & Metalcrafts, and Maison Royale, sifting through chests, consoles, benches, stools, and mantles. The tight-knit bunch of specialty shop owners who masterfully and elegantly balanced competition and camaraderie couldn't help. The marbled box that Jourdan described was nowhere to be found.

With one week to go, the deadline to reverse the curse loomed, as did Lafitte's court arraignment. They still had a dozen other shops to search. And still no sign of Marie Laveau.

"We must find the jewels. I cannot go back to *The Pride* for eternity." Lafitte hovered at the bar while Juliet and Derek closed up after the last customers left. "We must go tonight and look again. I shall find us an oil lantern while the sky is dark."

"It's 3:00 in the morning. The shops are closed," Juliet groaned and raked her fingers through her blonde hair. "I'm tired. Some idiot spilled beer all over me. I wanna take a shower and go to bed."

"I can search without you," he replied. "I am a pirate. There is no treasure I cannot find."

"No," Juliet said. "You're not allowed out of my sight. Do you wanna get arrested again?"

"I suppose not," Lafitte sighed and leaned against the bar. "I cannot waste more time in gaol."

"Though I'm sure y'all'd fit right in with all the crazies in there," Derek added. He scowled as he held a stack of receipts and punched codes into the register. In the dim house lights, Juliet swept the floor.

Juliet held her broom toward Lafitte. "You could at least help us clean so we can get out of here sooner."

"I do not swab the deck!" Lafitte stood upright and puffed out his chest. "I am the captain of *The Pride*. The captain does not *swab*."

"This is not a ship." Juliet jabbed him in the ribs with the end of the broom. "Help us or else."

"Or else what?"

"Or else I'll make you walk the plank." Juliet got right up in his face and grabbed the collar of his red cloak. "Dead men tell no tales."

Listening to their tête-à-tête, Derek laughed out loud. "Jules, we don't have a plank."

"You're supposed to have my six," Juliet half-sneered and half-laughed, letting go of Lafitte's collar. She was thankful to have Derek, and Leah for that matter, as good friends. They made working at the bar bearable, especially on late nights like this.

"Girl, you know I do." He glanced at Lafitte. "He can walk you home and I can get back to Aneeka and the twins. Maybe only one of them will be up tonight." He wiped his bald head with a thick hand. "I spent years throwin' drunks out of rowdy bars, but my kids have them all beat. Those two could break anyone."

Juliet walked into the back room. As she wiped down the piano and blew out the candles, the phantom red eyes in the corner stared back at her, sending a chill up her spine. She closed her eyes, willing them to go away. When she looked back again, they were gone.

"Those eyes..." she called to the men. "They're back again."

"As long as a head doesn't form around them, I'd say you're safe," Derek said.

"Not funny."

"I shall protect you, belle gosse." Jean Lafitte unsheathed his sword, raised it in front of Juliet, and slashed the empty air in front of them.

After the trio was done cleaning, Derek locked the door. As they stood on the sidewalk, Juliet huffed. "I'm beat. These late nights are killer. Derek, I don't know how you do it."

"You get used to it after a while," he said.

"I doubt it."

Lafitte held his elbow for Juliet. "Are you ready, belle gosse?"

She chuckled at his valiant gesture, nodded, and took his arm. "Despite what the other pirates think, maybe you're a softie after all."

"What is a softie?" he asked.

"A man with no cajones," Derek laughed.

"And... we're out of here." Juliet guided Jean Lafitte northeast on Bourbon Street toward Marigny. "Goodnight Derek. See you tomorrow night."

Chapter 23

The next day, Juliet woke up right before noon to find Jean Lafitte hovering near her bed. She scrambled to pull the covers up over her tank top and shorts, and shrieked, "I told you you weren't allowed in my room! Get out!"

"But we must keep looking for the sapphires. We have one week to find them." He stood fully dressed, down to his boots. "And we still need to search for the rubies. Their whereabouts are unknown."

"Yes, I get it. But get out of my room!" She held the sheets against her with one hand and jerked a finger to her door with the other.

"Make haste!" Lafitte turned and exited.

"You're killin' me, Smalls," Juliet muttered to herself. As she got dressed in jeans and a Nirvana T-shirt, she reflected on how her life had changed over the past week. For someone who initially got under her skin and scared the bejeezus out of her, she had grown to appreciate Jean Lafitte. His madness and brilliance intrigued her. He was still a lecherous marauder, but he had his chivalrous moments.

Moments later, she found him in her front room, ready to leave.

"I need coffee first." Stepping in front of Lafitte, Juliet headed out the door with him on her heels.

A half mile later, they found themselves outside of CC's Coffee House on the upper end of Royal Street. The three-story cotton-candy-colored building invited them in. Jean Lafitte stretched his neck upward at the empty second-story gallery and squinted.

"What's up there?" Juliet asked.

"Two young children in dressing gowns," he said, frowning. "Laughing at me."

Juliet didn't have the time or effort to bother with the young ghosts. "Ignore them. Let's go." She led him into the coffee shop.

"What can I get for you, darlin'?" the squat woman behind the counter asked her.

"A grande café au lait, please." Juliet eyed the croissants and muffins in the glass case in front of her.

"Something to eat too?" the woman asked.

"Not today."

"Okay, darlin', give me a minute and I'll get your drink." She turned away.

Lafitte whispered in Juliet's ear, "You did not wish to eat?"

She spoke low, "Mine are better." Realizing what she said, she cringed that she couldn't take it back. Her mother taught her that baking was subjective and every palate was different.

"Perhaps you should work here and bring your knowledge?" he offered.

Juliet looked around the cute café. A few people gathered at the round tables chatting and eating. "The hours would be better, that's for sure. And no one would spill beer on me." She tipped her head upward toward the ceiling. "Hopefully the ghosts only stay on the second floor."

The barista called, interrupting them, "Grande café au lait."

With a drink in hand, Juliet led Jean Lafitte down Royal Street. The mid-day sun warmed the mid-October day as tourists meandered in and out of art galleries and clothing boutiques. Juliet and Lafitte crossed Dumaine, St. Ann, and St. Peter Streets. Two blocks later, they passed the courthouse. NOPD watched them, mounted on horses. Juliet discreetly looked for Officer Martinez. Maybe in a couple more weeks, she told herself.

On the next block, Juliet stopped in her tracks, Lafitte nearly stumbling into her. "I can't believe I forgot about this place." Tourists wandered around them on Royal Street, noshing on pastries from across the street at Café Beignet.

"What place?"

"Keil's."

Large, forest green awnings decorated the sidewalk-level windows of the three-story red brick antique shop. Massive glass and bronze lanterns flanked the edges of the store that shared the block with other antique proprietors. A metal fire escape connected the second and third floors above them. Keil's was a staple in New Orleans' antique market.

Lafitte followed Juliet through glass doors with iron fleurs de lis encased between. The whole shop was illuminated in a yellow haze from the dozens of gold and crystal chandeliers that hung from the ceiling. Cursing, Juliet knocked her knee into three bronze statues of Greek women dressed in togas that greeted them. Eighteenth- and nineteenth-century pieces of art, furniture, and jewelry were featured in the front room. The scent of old, rich, and well-oiled leather brought them back to another time.

Lafitte motioned to the brilliant lighting above them. "Those are worth a pretty penny. I can tell the crystals are real."

"Yep," Juliet replied. "Some sell for twenty thousand dollars now."

A middle-aged couple stood at the glass counter talking to a female antiquarian in a lavender dress. Juliet and Jean Lafitte tiptoed along the green carpet through display rooms filled with French provincial armoires, hand-carved mahogany bed sets, and intricate gold mirrors. They examined each wall searching for the box of jewels.

"I'm Roberta. May I help you?" The woman in the lavender dress approached them. Classy diamond earrings sparkled next to her auburn hair. Her makeup was soft and muted. She oozed Southern hospitality.

Startled, a slight gasp escaped Juliet's mouth as she turned to face the woman. Lafitte ignored them as he studied the base of a priceless grandfather clock along a nearby wall.

"Y-... Yes," Juliet stuttered. She pointed quickly at Jean Lafitte who had moved along the wall toward a French Mahogany Empire Console. "My friend and I are looking for something specific. A marble box. In a corner. We'd like to take a look at its contents."

"A marble box? You must be mistaken." Roberta's head flinched back slightly.

"I'm guessing it's about this big." Juliet held her hands a foot apart in front of her.

"We don't have anything like that for sale," Roberta said. "It's not for sale."

"But you do have it?"

"Well, yes." Roberta maneuvered around a 19th Century English Chippendale Mahogany Kidney Shaped Leather-Top Desk toward a corner. "Follow me. But I still think you're mistaken."

Lafitte joined the women as Roberta pointed to a small marble box nestled in a corner. A white cardboard tag attached to it said: "Not for Sale."

"This is it!" Lafitte fell to the wooden floor to grab it. Before he could pick it up, Roberta stopped him.

"You can't have it," she insisted as she held her hand up in a stopping motion.

"But it is mine," Lafitte answered. "The contents inside are mine. They were stolen from me."

"I don't think so," Roberta said. She shook her head at him.

"Huh?" Juliet interrupted. "What do you mean?"

Roberta bent down and pointed to the brass plate on the front of the marble box. "These are Bennie's ashes." The brass plate said: *Bennie Hensley. With loving memories Grand Pa. You will always be missed, but never forgotten.* Roberta stood and placed a hand on her hip, her lavender dress swayed slightly. "It's an urn for our dear friend Bennie. He was a porter here for almost 80 years. He passed away shortly after Katrina. He loved this shop. And has never left."

"There are no sapphires inside?" Lafitte wrinkled his nose at Roberta.

"Sapphires? No. Only ashes."

"But--" he started.

Realizing the mistake and before Lafitte caused a scene, Juliet grabbed him by the elbow. She said to Roberta, "I'm so sorry. We didn't mean to waste your time. You're so kind to help us." She guided Lafitte back through the maze of expensive furnishings leaving Roberta behind.

On the sidewalk, under the green awning, Lafitte scoffed and paced the cement like a caged animal. "Jourdan double-crossed us!"

"Yep, he did," Juliet spoke softly, trying in vain to deescalate Lafitte's anger. She reached for his arm, but he pulled away. She found the situation almost humorous. A ghost bested a cursed pirate while both were stuck in purgatory in present day. And a deceased porter's ashes were kept in an urn inside an antique shop for his eternal resting place. Because where else would they be? The city never ceased to amaze Juliet.

Lafitte's cheeks reddened and his dark eyes turned cold and hard. "He played me for a fool. No one plays Captain Jean Lafitte for a fool." A vein in his forehead pulsed. "He shall pay for this. If I only had a plank for him to walk. I would send him to Davy Jones' Locker!" He pounded his fist into the wooden post next to the entrance to Keil's. "I shall get revenge on him."

Chapter 24

"Let's get a drink and regather our thoughts," Juliet suggested. "I know a place you'll like. It's right around the corner." A cocktail in the middle of the day in The Quarter was not only expected, it was encouraged.

Lafitte snorted, but begrudgingly followed her. She needed a drink too.

They headed southwest on Royal Street. Juliet knew it wouldn't be worth her time to point anything interesting out because Jean Lafitte was in no mood. She could feel his hatred for Jourdan emanating from him. Relief rushed through her knowing that his vengeance was projected onto someone else. She didn't want to be on the receiving end of a sword. An NOPD officer trotted by on his horse. Juliet thought of Officer Martinez. The cute cop had unexpectedly calmed her when Lafitte raised her frustration temperature.

They made the first right onto Bienville Street, named after Jean-Baptiste Le Moyne de Bienville, an early governor of Louisiana. One block later, they arrived at their destination.

"Does this place look familiar?" Juliet asked as they stood in front of a two-story dingy-white building that had open doors on both sides of the corner block. Over each door, giant palladium windows were the only source of natural light on the first floor of the historic building. Not much had changed to the 300-year-old structure. White gauze spiderwebs hung from the second-floor balcony celebrating the Halloween season. Purple and orange string lights serpentined up the light post on the corner.

"'Tis where I struck a deal with Andrew Jackson," Lafitte replied. The hatred on his face slowly softened.

"So, the rumors are true?"

"Indeed." A hint of a smile formed under his handlebar mustache.

Juliet led him into Old Absinthe House. Inside, Lafitte gazed upward with sudden focus. His lips parted slightly. He had never seen anything so odd. From the ceiling hung dozens of football helmets from current and former NFL teams. The walls surrounding them were covered with random stickers, business cards, and pictures. A paint color could not be identified from the shroud of offbeat decorations.

"What are they?" He pointed upward.

Laughing, Juliet quickly explained modern football. "They are like helmets from a suit of armor."

"Aye." Lafitte saddled up to a stool at the bar and motioned for Juliet to join him. Patrons filled the bar around them in the center of the room.

The female bartender approached them. "What can I get for y'all?" She wore a black T-shirt and appeared to be in her fifties with a few wrinkles on her face and a paunchy stomach. Juliet guessed the woman had been tending bar for a couple of decades and she worried she would suffer the same fate. She still wished to get back into the pastry business.

"I shall have your finest rum," Lafitte answered, resting his fist on the bar.

"Comin' up. Say--" the barmaid said, noting Lafitte's attire, "you look like Jean Lafitte. Nice Halloween costume."

"I--" he started to say, but Juliet quickly elbowed him in the side and hushed him.

Juliet said, "He's a reenactor. I'm a bartender at Lafitte's Blacksmith Shop and he entertains our customers."

The woman nodded with approval. "Spittin' image." She turned to Juliet. "What would you like?"

"I'll have the same. I'm buying."

As the barmaid prepared their drinks, the room hummed with conversations of other patrons. Some watched the overhead TV while others added their playlist to the digital jukebox on the wall. A middle-aged couple entered the bar and took a seat next to Juliet. The husband wore a Boston Red Sox baseball hat that almost covered his white hair. The wife looked excited to be in a historic bar.

The husband said to his wife, "This bahr is wherah that pirate Black Beahd lost a gambling debt to Alexandah Hamilton."

Juliet chuckled quietly at the New Englander's ignorance of Louisiana history.

"It was not Black Beard," Jean Lafitte interrupted the man. "It was Jean Lafitte. The Captain of *The Pride*."

"That right?" the man countered, smiling wide in return. His wife turned toward the men, taking an interest in their conversation.

"Aye."

Juliet nudged Lafitte hoping that he would take the hint to not reveal his true self to these tourists.

Lafitte continued, "On the second floor of this--" he glanced around the grimy room, "*fine* establishment, Jean Lafitte secretly met with General Andrew Jackson during the War of 1812. Jackson struck a deal with me, er Lafitte, asking for assistance to defeat the British Navy. I, I mean he, only agreed if his band of pirates were released from prison. Jackson agreed and the Battle of New Orleans was fought on January 8, 1815. He provided the flints and the gunpowder from his stolen stores in Barataria. Some lives were lost, but the pirates and the Americans were victorious. President Madison later pardoned him."

"That's a great story," the man from New England said.

Juliet was proud of Lafitte for maintaining his alter-ego.

"However, it was all in vain," Lafitte explained. "The War of 1812 had officially ended when the Treaty of Ghent was signed two weeks prior. News did not travel quickly two hundred years ago. Your phones did not exist."

"You know your history," the barmaid said as she put two shots of rum in front of Jean Lafitte and Juliet.

"Aye, madam." He nodded to her and swallowed his rum in one gulp. "To toast the victory, the captain and his crew celebrated with raucous drinking on the second floor."

"That's right," the bartender said. "We sometimes hear strange sounds up there like there's a party happening. We'll go up there and find nothing."

"Your bar is haunted," Juliet said. "Just like mine."

"Isn't every bar in this city haunted?" the woman laughed.

* * * *

As Juliet nursed her second shot of rum, Lafitte's glass was already empty. He threw back alcohol like it was water. After being restricted on a ship for two hundred years with an endless supply, no wonder his tolerance was off the charts.

"I'm glad I brought you here," Juliet said. "You needed something to take your mind off Pierre Jourdan."

"What a rapscallion! He tried to hornswoggle me."

"He sent us on a wild goose chase," Juliet pointed out. "Sorry... do you know that phrase?"

"Of course! When I was in France, I studied Shakespeare." He jutted out his chest. "Nay, if thy wits run the wild-goose chase, I have done, for thou hast more of the wild-goose in one of thy wits than, I am sure, I have in my whole five."

"From *Romeo and--*"

"*--Juliet.*" Lafitte smiled wide at her. "Is this how you were named?"

Juliet nodded slowly. "My mother always wanted to go to Verona, but never got the chance." She missed her mother, but knew her mom would be proud. "Anyway, I wonder if Pierre Jourdan sent us to Keil's to keep us away from Muriel's? Maybe he has the sapphires there?"

"'Tis possible." Lafitte twirled his mustache between his fingers. "When I retrieved a booty when I knew other buccaneers searched for it, I sent them east if I was heading west."

Juliet pressed her fingers into her forehead. "But how do we get him to hand them over? The Lady of the Night wouldn't help us. He won't give them up without a fight." As her pulse quickened, so did her speech. "If we can't get the sapphires from him and the emeralds from The Lady of the Night, how on earth will we find the rubies? We have no idea where they are." Juliet took a breath from talking so fast. "And then you're stuck on your ship for eternity. But you have a court date next week. You could go to jail. And you still owe me money for posting bail. That was my savings. I'll never be a pastry chef again because I'll be stuck slinging drinks for the rest of my life."

"Easy, belle gosse." Lafitte stroked her forearm. "You are raising a white flag too soon."

"How can you be so sure?" Her green eyes widened at him. If it was another time and another place, she might have been interested in him. He was handsome in an unexpected way. Not like the obnoxious man-boys who hit on her at the tavern. Their fraternity antics annoyed her. But Lafitte wasn't like that. She waved off the amorous thoughts. They had a treasure to find!

"Because I am Jean Lafitte the Pirate, the Terror of the Gulf Coast!" he boasted, slapping a hand to his chest. "There is no treasure I cannot find. I shall retrieve these jewels and return them to Isla Mujeres."

"I think we'll need Madame Delia's help again."

Chapter 25

With three days to go, Juliet and Jean Lafitte entered Madame Delia's voodoo shop on St. Peter Street. The old woman was rolling a smudge stick when they walked in. An aroma of earthy incense filled the air. Her decorated beech walking cane rested against the counter. "You have returned for my help," she said, without looking up.

How the wrinkled soothsayer anticipated them, Juliet never knew.

"Yes, ma'am," Juliet said. Lafitte stood next to her, his arms across his chest.

"The Lady of the Night would not assist you," Madame Delia said, finally looking at them. "That was an unfortunate setback." Today, she wove a purple scarf through her hair and she wore a long flowing dress.

"She has my emeralds," Lafitte huffed.

"And we think Pierre Jourdan at Muriel's has the sapphires," Juliet added.

"We offered The Lady of the Night to Jourdan," Lafitte explained, "and he accepted in exchange for the sapphires, but she refused, and he double-crossed me anyway. He shall pay."

"What can you offer The Lady of the Night that she cannot refuse?" Madame Delia asked in more of a statement than a question.

"No idea." Juliet shrugged.

"Everyone has their breaking point. You have to find it." Behind the counter, the old woman rested against her walking cane.

"She refused the trinkets we offered her and I don't have the money to buy real stuff," Juliet said. She eyed Lafitte's gold-handled cutlass that hung from his waist sash. He would never part with it, not even to save himself.

"The answer is not a treasure," Madame Delia replied. Her silver eyes glistened at them.

"What is it?" Lafitte demanded.

"Patience, Captain," Madame Delia spoke low. Her voice rippled like small waves throughout her shop.

"My patience has gone to the bottom of the ocean!" he shouted, rattling the gris-gris hanging on a nearby wall. "I have three days to find the jewels or I will be stuck here for eternity!"

"You must discover the answers for yourselves," the old woman instructed.

He huffed and placed a hand on his sword.

Noticing his desire to fight, Juliet grabbed him by the arm and said, "Let's get outta here and go back to MRB." She thanked the oracle on their way out.

On the sidewalk minutes later, Juliet reprimanded Jean Lafitte. "You can't pull your sword every time someone makes you angry. You'll go to jail for sure and never get out of here."

"But she would not answer me." He spoke through gritted teeth. "She is like the Sphinx."

"It's okay. We'll figure it out," Juliet assured him. "Let's go find The Lady of the Night."

Ten minutes later, they sauntered through the mossy-green doors of MRB. A handful of patrons downed the Green Drank while a few others chowed on po boys.

Juliet still didn't know what to offer The Lady of the Night. The ghostly woman couldn't use money or any kind of social media plug. It's not like she needed some followers or a good review written. Juliet couldn't help her go viral. Juliet was at a loss, but they needed an answer soon because Lafitte's deadline was fast approaching.

Rock music blared through overhead speakers as Juliet and Jean Lafitte made their way to the ladies' room.

"I have waited long enough," Lafitte snarled. "She must help us. I cannot go empty-handed back to *The Pride* when the moon is full in three nights." He heavily breathed through his nose, ready to lash out. He glared at everyone around him, anxious for answers.

"I get it. Don't freak out on me. You need this." A small smile formed on Juliet's face. She had to convince him this would work even if she might not believe it herself. The past week-and-a-half had been adventurous for her. Sure, she had lost her job at Willa Jean because of that ill-fated food critic, and the late nights at the tavern were killer on her sleep schedule. This time with Jean Lafitte would last her through any more obstacles that would come her way. Juliet would never forget it. And she would never forget Jean Lafitte. Despite what he claimed, in her eyes, he was *not* the Terror of the Gulf Coast. Then, to be safe, Juliet was careful not to wear any of her good, sparkly jewelry around The Lady of the Night. She wasn't taking any chances.

The ladies' room was empty, except for an excessive chill. The hairs on Juliet's arm stood up. She clutched Lafitte's arm as she trailed behind him.

"Good evening, m'lady." Breaking Juliet's hold, Lafitte stepped forward into the empty space, removed his tricorn hat, and bowed.

"How dare you come back," a bodiless voice echoed around them.

Juliet swallowed hard, afraid of what The Lady of the Night would do this time.

"I have come to discuss a negotiation with you," Lafitte said.

"I am listening," the bodiless voice said.

"Show yourself first," Lafitte instructed. "I need to see you."

Gradually, The Lady of the Night formed into an apparition in front of them. Her white gown floated around her, giving her an angelic, yet smoky, glow.

Lafitte spoke again, "I must apologize for my initial proposition of offering you up to the Frenchman. You are not a trollop."

"Keep going," The Lady of the Night said.

"You are a force," Lafitte said, "like the strongest wave in the ocean."

Juliet wasn't sure where he was headed in his monologue, but she stayed quiet next to him.

He took a step forward. "I need you. As my First Mate."

"You want me to be a pirate like you?" she hissed. "Pirates are liars and thieves."

"Aye," he said. "But as my First Mate, you can share the treasure. 'Tis called No Prey, No Pay. I did not pay my crew when we recovered a stolen bounty from a rival ship, but they received part of the loot."

Juliet wondered why Lafitte was bartering the jewels that he wanted, but she did not interrupt. She stood near the hand dryer as she watched them strike a deal.

"But I already have the emeralds," The Lady of the Night countered. "The jewels *you* want."

"How did you acquire them?" Lafitte wanted to know. The answer had been plaguing him since the first time he stepped into MRB. "Marie Laveau stole them from me."

"You are familiar with my reputation?" The Lady of the Night asked.

Remembering the apparition's habit, Juliet tugged on her earrings making sure they were still there.

"Aye," Lafitte said. "You like to take beautiful jewelry."

"That is how I came to have them." A wicked smile formed on her ghostly face.

"You stole them?" He asked in more of a statement than a question.

"What do you think?"

"Let's trade," Lafitte offered. He twirled his bushy mustache between his fingers.

"A trade?"

"Aye," he said, his voice smooth like the pearl of an oyster. "Your emeralds for sapphires." He stared at her ghostly face. "Like the stunning blue eyes you once had."

"My lover told me he got lost in them," she mused. "He called me his blue angel." She gazed down for a moment, recalling the fond memory, then raised her head back up. "I am interested in the sapphires you speak of."

"If you help me retrieve them, they are yours," Lafitte said.

"Where are they?" she asked.

"With Pierre Jourdan at Muriel's Restaurant."

"Pierre Jourdan?!" The Lady of the Night shrieked, causing the mirror above the bathroom sink to shatter. "That haughty Frenchman is a pigeon-livered ratbag!"

In the corner, Juliet choked on a laugh at the antiquated insult.

"Be quiet!" The Lady of the Night yelled at Juliet.

"You have heard of him?" Lafitte coyly asked.

"Heard of him?" The Lady of the Night sneered. "I despise him!" Her ghostly teeth bared and she lurched forward, causing Juliet to stumble back.

"Why do you hate him?" Juliet finally spoke. This sudden change of emotion from the apparition piqued her interest.

"He is a thief!" she snarled, causing the faucets to turn on full blast.

"What did he steal?" Juliet sidestepped the bouncing water, not seeing any pilfered jewelry The Lady of the Night had swiped from unsuspecting tourists over the years. Surely, Jourdan didn't steal the trinkets. Or did he?

"Clientele."

"Clientele?" Juliet and Lafitte gawped in unison.

"Yes," The Lady of the Night replied. "Look around. This establishment is sparsely full. I am tethered here for eternity watching patrons go in and out. But Pierre Jourdan has his own dining table. Tourists flock to his restaurant, hoping to see him. He has stolen all of the people who used to come here, who used to frequent other premises in the French Quarter as well. Many of us hate him."

"If you help us defeat Pierre Jourdan and bring more people here, will you give us the emeralds?" Juliet asked, stepping next to Jean Lafitte.

The Lady of the Night nodded. "I can help you build a crew. Meet me tomorrow at midnight at Pirates Alley with Pierre Jourdan and the jewels. I will bring my allies and the emeralds."

Chapter 26

The next morning, rain fell in the Marigny with a slow gentle beat that fit perfectly into the ambiance of the mystical neighborhood. A few locals under umbrellas dodged their way around puddles along Burgundy Street. Days like this were an unexpected change, opening up the city to its natural assets of empty sidewalks, sending crowds of tourists inside.

Mesmerized by the uninterrupted cadence, Juliet gazed out the window of her front room. She had some time before she had to get ready for work. The rain reminded her of a famous quote by Tennessee Williams, an adopted son of The Big Easy: *Don't you just love those long rainy afternoons in New Orleans when an hour isn't just an hour - but a little piece of eternity dropped into your hands - and who knows what to do with it?*

"What are you watching, belle gosse?" Jean Lafitte asked from behind her. He stopped a few feet from her, admiring the curves of her body. He had come to respect her, but her loveliness still stopped him cold though he didn't understand the T-shirts she wore. Today it was Blondie. He knew he couldn't have Juliet, at least not this week. Time was running out and he still had jewels to find.

"Nothing, just the rain. I could watch it all day," she sighed, without looking at him. "It's cool now, because it's fall, but in the summer, when it's scorching hot out and I feel like I'm walking through Jell-O, I want to be outside in the warm rain when everyone else runs for cover. We walk slow because it's hard to move fast in the awful humidity."

"'Tis lovely," he said. "Like you."

Still facing away, a grin formed on Juliet's face. She liked the compliment. It felt nice. Nice in a non-creepy way. She would miss the marauder, no matter what happened after the full moon appeared in two nights. His arraignment was the next afternoon. But she knew he was still a deceitful, thieving pirate.

"You lied to The Lady of the Night," Juliet said, still watching the rain. She had to remind herself that his lies were part of being a pirate. It was part of the job description. She wasn't a prude, but had to go along with him.

"Aye."

"You told her she could have the sapphires. Sapphires you didn't have."

"She did not know that. I did what I had to do to assure the agreement." He crossed his arms over his chest.

Juliet finally turned around to face him. Her green eyes met his. "You're a liar and a thief."

"Aye." He bowed slightly to her.

She shook her head at him. "You're lucky she changed her attitude when you mentioned Pierre Jourdan. Otherwise, we would've been shit outta luck."

He gave her a funny look at the unfamiliar reference.

"Never mind." Juliet flicked a hand at him.

Lafitte then said, "We shall find out who The Lady of the Night has recruited tonight to assist us against Jourdan."

"But I have to go to work today," she said. "And you need to come with me."

"Aye, belle gosse."

Juliet took a step away from him to grab an umbrella from her coat closet.

"Incidentally," Lafitte asked, as they headed out the door, "what is Jell-O?"

* * * *

At Lafitte's Blacksmith Shop, they found Leah and Derek prepping for the day. Derek mopped the front entrance, wiping up errant wet footprints from the rain, in between dabbing the sweat from his bald head. Leah checked the bottle inventory to make sure nothing mysteriously broke overnight.

"What's the deets on the cursed jewels?" Derek asked them. "I came in early today because Aneeka'll quiz me when I get home. She's *obsessed* with this whole treasure hunt y'all have goin' on here. Like binge-watchin' a show in real life."

"My Mamere Essie, too," Leah added with a grin.

As she pulled chairs down from tables and set them up, Juliet filled Derek and Leah in about the deal they made with The Lady of the Night and her hatred for Pierre Jourdan.

"Who's her crew?" Leah wanted to know as she filled the ice bin.

"No idea." Juliet shrugged.

"We shall find out tonight," Jean Lafitte answered, standing in the middle of the room.

"Make yourself useful," Leah said and handed him a clean cloth to wipe down the bar.

When he gave her a look of righteous indignation, Juliet shot him a glare with daggers for eyes. He might be a Captain on *The Pride* and order his pirates around, but not while he was on land with her.

"Very well, belle gosse," he huffed and snatched the cloth out of Leah's hand.

As Lafitte buffed the bar, Juliet went into the back room to open the old window shutters. The rain outside puttered out as the sun poked through the clouds. The beginnings of a rainbow spread over the northeast corner of the French Quarter. Juliet smiled at the welcome weather change.

When she turned around, the phantom red eyes glared back at her from the corner. The hairs on her arm stood stiff at attention and a shudder coursed through her. She sucked in a deep gasp and closed her eyes. When she opened them, the supernatural pair was gone.

Leah came into the room, her long curly hair bounced against her shoulders as she walked. "Y'all okay, Jules? You look like you've seen a ghost."

"Uh- I- I don't know what I saw," Juliet puffed out, keeping her back to the wall. "Those red eyes... What are they? Who are they?"

"Nobody knows." Leah slung an arm around her friend's shoulder, but still stood upright as her proud grandmother had taught her. "As long as they don't do anythin' else, I think you'll be fine. Or like my Mamere Essie says, don't mind them and they don't mind you. My friend Melinda spent the night in one of those boutique hotels on Esplanade. She was doing some work at the desk and saw out of the corner of her eye the bed sink down as if someone had sat on it. No one else was in the room. Freaked her out a little, but she said out loud, 'I'll do me and you do you,' and she was fine."

Juliet offered a slight grin to her friend. "Good for her, but those red eyes still give me the creeps."

Chapter 27

At the end of her shift, Juliet and Jean Lafitte headed to Muriel's at the corner of St. Ann and Chartres. They didn't have a dinner reservation because the place was packed but detoured to the century-old Indoor Courtyard Bar. Juliet bought two drinks, a Ramos Gin Fizz for her and rum on the rocks for Lafitte, and they climbed the stairs to the Séance Lounge.

"We have a few hours before we meet The Lady of the Night in Pirates Alley," Juliet kept her voice low as they crested the steps. "What's your plan with Pierre Jourdan? He thinks he led us to Keil's. You can't let him know you're pissed about that. And he thinks he's getting The Lady of the Night."

"Do not worry, belle gosse," Lafitte smirked, waving a dismissive hand at her. "My plans never fail."

When they entered the Séance Lounge, they saw a few customers relaxing on the velvet chaises, sipping drinks.

"What do we do now?" Juliet spoke out of the side of her mouth to Lafitte. "They can't be here." She swallowed her cocktail.

"I shall take care of it," he said, gulping down his rum.

Stepping toward the small group, Jean Lafitte removed his tricorn hat and bowed to them, whisking his red velvet cloak behind him. "Are you here waiting to see Pierre Jourdan?"

The man sitting between two women spoke, "Yeah, we wanna catch a ghost in action." He held up a fancy camera that he held on his lap.

Lafitte glanced around the room and frowned. "I do not see him. Perhaps you shall have better luck elsewhere?"

"We heard this is the best place in town to find a ghost," the woman on the right said. "I can't wait to tell my friends back home I saw one."

Juliet remembered what The Lady of the Night had said about Pierre Jourdan stealing all of the tourists. It was apparently true.

"I can present a better offer to you," Lafitte said to the customers. "If you leave now, I promise you shall see plenty in Pirates Alley at midnight. You shall be rewarded handsomely."

"Eh, we've been waiting here for an hour and haven't seen anything," the second woman said. "Let's get outta here."

The trio downed their drinks and headed out.

After they left, Juliet turned to Lafitte, "How do you do that? How do you get normal people to do what you want?"

"I am a Captain." He stood tall, with his hands on his hips. "'Tis in my blood. If they do not, I make them walk the plank."

Juliet shook her head and smiled. His cockiness never ceased to amaze her. She stepped away from him and studied the empty room. "Monsieur Jourdan, are you here?"

"You have returned," a bodiless voice echoed around them. "Did you bring The Lady of the Night to be my companion?"

"Um, not exactly," Juliet answered. She locked eyes with Jean Lafitte, sending him a nervous glance, hoping her next statement would be believed. "She agreed to meet you, tonight at midnight, in Pirates Alley."

"Splendid." With that, Pierre Jourdan appeared before them, slowly transitioning from a transparent apparition to a near-human. He stood at the thick maroon velvet drapes that cinched at the wall that separated the two rooms of the lounge.

"She agreed to meet you," Lafitte explained, "on one condition."

"What is that?" Jourdan asked.

"That you bring the sapphires."

The haughty Frenchman laughed, his howl reverberating through the room. "I see that you did not find them in the marble box."

"No," Juliet deadpanned. "It was an urn full of a dead man's ashes." She was not amused by his arrogance. Typical for a Frenchman.

"You purposely led us on a wild goose chase."

"Guilty," Jourdan smirked as if it wasn't a big deal that he wasted their time. He laughed again. "Tell me why I should bring the sapphires to The Lady of the Night."

"Because she does not come free," Lafitte stated.

Juliet almost choked on the double entendre, but held her composure.

"And," Lafitte continued, "she knows of other priceless jewels. Emeralds and rubies. They could be yours. Rubies are worth ten times more than sapphires alone."

Another lie, Juliet thought to herself. But she kept quiet, knowing that Lafitte's false statement was for the greater good of their search for the cursed jewels. The fine line between honesty and deception was getting dangerously thin.

"Interesting," Jourdan mused. He cupped his chin with his hand and tapped his index finger along his chin. "Rubies are indeed priceless."

Juliet purposely bit her lip, so as not to cause doubt. She knew they had no idea where to find the rubies.

Lafitte spoke, a wide smile forming under his bushy mustache, "They could all be yours tonight."

"Yes," Jourdan said. "I shall do it. I shall bring the sapphires to The Lady of the Night tonight at midnight in exchange for rubies and emeralds."

Juliet glanced at her phone. It was 10:00. They had two hours to go. This rendezvous could go very well or extremely bad. She hoped for the former. With all her internal might, Juliet willed The Lady of the Night to deliver what she promised. Juliet hoped for a speedy arraignment for Jean Lafitte the next day and then he would be on his way to Isla Mujeres with the jewels. And then her life would be back to normal. Did she want that? She wasn't sure.

Then Lafitte held out his right hand to the Frenchman. "We are in agreement?"

Jourdan shook his hand and disappeared into the air before them.

* * * *

Juliet and Jean Lafitte headed northwest on St. Ann Street. Pirates Alley was one block to the left on the other side of The Presbytère, the now state museum that held Mardi Gras exhibits in the palatial former 19th Century courthouse.

At the next corner, Lafitte stopped abruptly, causing Juliet to bump into him. He stared at the inky sky.

"What is it?" she asked, looking up into the empty sky. Only a nearby lamp post provided light for her.

"They are here," he said. "The Lady of the Night fulfilled her promise." He grasped her hand, and like before, Juliet could now see the apparitions that he saw. Above them, white apparitions floated over the black iron railings attached to the surrounding buildings. Dozens of them hovered back and forth, like sheets of floating milky fabric. It was hard to tell where one ended and another began. They reminded her of the Dementors in *Harry Potter*, only pale instead of black.

At this time of night, this end of The Quarter was deserted. Most of the inebriated travelers were at the other end of Bourbon Street listening to bar bands, getting entertained by street performers, or people-watching. Those who wandered about here didn't notice the spectacle above them.

"Whoa," Juliet spoke barely above a whisper. She swallowed hard and gripped Lafitte's hand. Even though she had encountered single ghosts with Lafitte, the group of spirits above her left her in awe. Her shoulders raised and she stared unabashedly upward. She almost forgot to blink.

They made a left on Royal, weaving their way around the nocturnal crowds who had no patience for the drunk tourists on Bourbon a block away. The black streetlamps guided their way along the narrow, gray sidewalk. Most of the antique galleries and boutiques had closed their doors hours ago, but adjoining restaurants were filled with twilight patrons. The street artists who hawked their wares during the day along the black wrought iron fence surrounding St. Anthony's Garden had packed up long ago.

Behind St. Louis Cathedral, the garden proudly presented "Touchdown Jesus." St. Anthony's Garden was once a popular place for duels near the local priest to give last rights to the loser. These days, the quiet, serene garden was fenced off to tourists and vagrants. The grassy courtyard still housed a few statues and monuments, the tallest being a twenty-foot cement obelisk. A few yards away, and half the size, an unobtrusive Tuscan marble statue of Jesus raised his hands in praise. During Hurricane Katrina, the figure lost a forefinger and a thumb.

Now, after the sun went down and a forward-thinking electrician purposely directed some spotlights, it was evident how the statue earned its moniker. The shadow of the effigy almost reached the roof of the colossal French Neo-Gothic church. Jesus could be seen from the next block signaling a touchdown.

Juliet swallowed hard. "I wonder if Touchdown Jesus'll ward off the bad demons. And only keep the good ones?"

"'Tis hard to say, belle gosse. I have never seen such a spectacle." The spirits in the sky circled the church, but none descended toward them. "I do not see The Lady of the Night."

"We're early," Juliet said. "She might not be here for another hour. Maybe she's busy swiping bracelets from unsuspecting women at MRB."

Chapter 28

At 11:00, the moon, although massive in the sky, was two days short of being completely full. The alabaster spirits floated in the night, creating a haze. Only a handful of street lamps illuminated the otherwise dark area. Juliet and Jean Lafitte waited for The Lady of the Night and Pierre Jourdan at the entrance to Pirates Alley intersecting the 700 block of Royal Street. The thin strip of slate sidewalk separated the cathedral from shops, rumored-to-be-haunted Faulkner House Books, and Pirate's Alley Café.

Local legend stated that the alley earned its name from the influx of pirates in the 1700s who entered the city from the Mississippi River a quarter-mile away. These days, a chaplain married couples with a quick elopement in the infamous snicket-way.

If all went well tonight, Juliet and Lafitte would recover two of the three pairs of jewels. But where was the third? They had scoured the French Quarter over the past 12 days and didn't find any hint of where the rubies could be. Nor had anyone they had encountered mentioned the missing gems. With just over 48 hours to go, Juliet doubted they'd find the rubies in time for Lafitte's curse to be broken. Damn Marie Laveau!

But he didn't seem worried. Steps away from her, he practiced his sword dueling techniques with his gold-handled cutlass. He parried and jumped along the slate squares, pretending to jab an enemy.

Juliet wondered why he prepared like that. It wasn't as though he could kill Pierre Jourdan if something went south. The man was already dead. Maybe Lafitte knew something she didn't.

"How much longer, belle gosse?" Lafitte asked as he lunged in a mock riposte.

"Another hour."

"We shall be victorious tonight!" he called, without looking back to her. His sword whisped through the air, decapitating a few of the low-hanging tree branches that sagged over the black fence surrounding St. Anthony's Garden. "If I only had my pistol. I could be doubly armed."

"You don't even know if Pierre Jourdan will attack," Juliet half-scoffed, half-laughed.

"'Tis better to be prepared to face an adversary than not, belle gosse." He parried again and bounced along the slate sidewalk.

"If you hadn't threatened that NOPD cop with your gun, you would have it."

"Lesson learned." He spoke as if he had done something as simple as knowing not to touch a hot stove after he scorched a finger.

"Don't forget, your arraignment is tomorrow morning."

"Aye. I shall not forget."

"Even though this is named Pirates Alley, did you ever do business here?"

"No. T'was too risky. Look around." He pointed to the surrounding structures with his sword. "A state building, an old parish prison, and a cathedral. Not a good place for a buccaneer like me. The authorities would have instantly arrested me and thrown me in gaol. Or the governor would have had my head. My brother, who gave me this sword, was not as fortunate. He was arrested and spent a steaming summer in chains in Jackson Square."

Juliet glanced down Royal Street, watching for The Lady of the Night and her entourage. Would the spirits circling above them descend to join them? But then again, would Juliet see her without physically touching Jean Lafitte? Probably not. That new ability to catch sight of ghosts still blew Juliet's mind. The Quarter had human *and* just as many non-human residents. But, she suspected, once Lafitte left in two nights, that she would lose her knack to watch the undead. Being a voyeur in a haunted city had its privileges. Even if it was only temporary.

If nothing else, being around Jean Lafitte gave Juliet the confidence to bake a King Cake again. She hadn't attempted to make the crown jewel concoction since she was fired from Willa Jean last month. It would have to wait until next week. Right now, she had a ghost face-off to behold. The situation was risky since she and Lafitte had no idea how it would turn out, but the payout of two pairs of jewels was worth it.

Lafitte finished practicing his swordsmanship, sheathed his weapon, and positioned himself next to Juliet. He grabbed her hand.

Twenty yards ahead of them, an otherwise dark Royal Street lit up with The Lady of the Night and her legion. Their forms were ethereal, with translucent silhouettes suspended in the air. Faint wisps of mist swirled around the small army, creating an aura of mystery and unease. Juliet could almost see through them as if they existed in a realm between the tangible and the intangible. The Lady of the Night commandeered thirty others behind her, her ivory dress flowing like a warrior queen.

Time stood still as Juliet locked her eyes on these otherworldly beings. A mix of fear, fascination, and curiosity coursed through her. She had seen ghosts this week, but nothing like this. Every nerve in her body tingled with a mixture of trepidation and awe. It was a sight that defied explanation, challenging the boundaries of her understanding of reality. Good thing these specters were on her and Jean Lafitte's side.

As the spooky group marched toward them, the light across the street sizzled out.

The Lady of the Night spoke, "Good evening. We are ready."

Lafitte stepped in front of Juliet, still holding her hand. "Who is your crew?" He glanced behind their leader at her ragtag gang. Above them, the floating apparitions came to a stop, as if watching the scene below.

"I've brought everyone who has been slighted by Pierre Jourdan." She gestured to several Black ghosts to her right. "Beginning with the slaves from the LaLaurie Mansion." Juliet remembered hearing about them from the ghost tour the previous week. They carried the weight of a painful past. The ghosts' eyes, though intangible, conveyed the depth of despair and longing for freedom. Their forms were forever caught between the realm of the living and the afterlife, perpetually reliving the trauma and injustices of their existence. Occasionally, they quivered behind their leader, as though they expected to be chased down again by their former master.

Juliet bit her bottom lip, but didn't say anything. She gripped Lafitte's hand harder.

The Lady of the Night spoke again, "Beside them is the Octoroon Mistress and General Beauregard." She pointed to a naked woman and a man in a decorated gray soldier's uniform and stocking feet.

Legend had it that the Octoroon Mistress was well-known at 734 Royal Street. Being one-eighth Black, the girl found her demise on the rooftop of the house on the other side of St. Anthony's Garden one cold December night in the 1850s. She had fallen in love with a rich and handsome Frenchman but, because she was of mixed race, he would not marry her. To prove her undying love, she stripped naked and waited for him on the roof while he entertained friends. He forgot about her and, the next morning, found her frozen to death. She haunted the residence ever since.

P. G. T. Beauregard was one of the first and most respected generals of the Confederate Army. He had rented a bright yellow house on nearby 1113 Chartres Street in 1865. Even though had only lived there for 18 months, he still lingered there in the afterlife. At the now-named Beauregard-Keyes House, he poked around at night looking for his boots. It seems they buried the man in his stocking feet and, being a meticulous dresser, especially in uniform, he could not rest until he found them.

The Lady of the Night gestured to the spirits hovering above them. "And these are from the Mahogany Jazz Club and Arnaud's."

"Welcome," Jean Lafitte said to all of them with a grand sweeping motion of his free arm. He still held Juliet's hand with his other. "My regards for your assistance." He turned to The Lady of the Night. "You have a fine crew. Do you have the emeralds?"

She reached into the folds of her pale dress and presented the pair of sparkling jewels. Their green essence cast radiant prisms along her otherwise ashen face.

"They are exactly like I remember them," Lafitte mused. "You shall get what I promised."

"They are yours when we take down Pierre Jourdan," The Lady of the Night hissed. "And not before." She shoved them back into the hidden pockets of her skirt. "You are still a pirate and I cannot fully trust you."

With her free hand, Juliet pulled her phone out of her pocket and glanced at the time. "It's almost midnight. Jourdan should be here soon."

The bell on the clock of nearby St. Louis Cathedral bonged.

Chapter 29

The sound of boots clapped against the slate sidewalk, increasing in sound as Pierre Jourdan approached. Juliet held her breath, willing this night to go smoothly. Even though it was late, and she should have been asleep in her comfy bed, adrenaline pumped through her veins. Nervous, she bounced from foot to foot.

"It is midnight," Pierre Jourdan announced to the group. He still wore the tuxedo that Juliet and Jean Lafitte met him the first time at Muriel's. He scraped a ghostly hand along his head. "I'd like to see the other jewels you promised me."

"Not so fast," Lafitte commanded, taking a step forward. "Show us the sapphires first."

Jourdan scoffed in cocky amusement, glanced at Juliet, and back to Lafitte. "Very well." He reached into his pocket and pulled out two sparkling blue gems. Their brilliance reminded Juliet of the turquoise Caribbean. Their enchanting beauty captivated her gaze. They nestled between Jourdan's fingers, boasting a deep azure hue reminiscent of a vast ocean, evoking a sense of tranquility and mystery. Their surface danced with flecks of lighter blues, reminiscent of sunlight refracting on gentle waves. No wonder Jean Lafitte was mesmerized by them and their powers.

Lafitte locked eyes with The Lady of the Night as if they shared a secret, then turned back to Jourdan. "She has the pair of emeralds." Her army of apparitions stood sentry behind her.

"I would like to see them," Jourdan said flatly. "Quid pro quo."

Lafitte nodded to her.

The Lady of the Night presented the precious green stones. Each emerald glistened and glimmered, emanating a mesmerizing green hue that danced in the dim light of Pirates Alley. The illumination interacted with their facets, creating a play of shadows and reflections that added to their allure. The energy they emitted seemed to flow through her hand, carrying a sense of vitality and renewal.

Lafitte spoke again, "Let us hand the stones to my First Mate." He gestured to Juliet with his free hand, while gripping her other. While protecting her, he did not want to let go of her for fear she would miss something. "She is an objective third party who can hold them until we reach an agreement."

"I disagree," Jourdan volleyed with a wide stance. "She is with you. How can she be objective?"

"She is not a ghost," Lafitte answered. "Nor a pirate like me. She has my trust and she should have yours too."

Pierre Jourdan twisted his lips together with a slight frown. "Hmmm."

"I trust her," The Lady of the Night said. She placed her emeralds into Juliet's free hand. "She has gained my trust this past week. She means me no harm."

Juliet smiled at the compliment. She still couldn't believe this scene was unfolding around her. If only she could get her phone out to snap a photo to prove to Leah and Derek, but she didn't want to disrupt anything.

The Lady of the Night spoke again, "But you..." She nodded toward Lafitte. "You are a pirate who cannot be trusted."

"Remember our agreement," he warned her. "You shall be rewarded handsomely."

Jourdan said, "And what about me?"

"I had a feeling you would be hesitant," Lafitte said. "And because of that, I have a counteroffer."

"I'm listening." Jourdan leaned close to Lafitte. His eyes widened with anticipation. As did The Lady of the Night.

"What is better than a pair of sapphires?" Lafitte asked him.

"Ten sapphires?" Jourdan answered.

"Wrong," Lafitte chuckled, his mouth curling upward into a grin.

"Wrong?" Jourdan said, tilting his head and narrowing his eyes.

Discreetly squeezing Juliet's hand, Lafitte said, "Ten *thousand* sapphires are better than a pair." He smiled wide and Juliet understood what he was doing.

"Where do you have ten thousand sapphires?" Jourdan wanted to know. "Surely not here."

"Correct," Lafitte replied. "Not here. You shall come with me to my ship, *The Pride*. My crew and I have plans to travel to Isla Mujeres where these sapphires originated. The island holds a king's ransom of sapphires, emeralds, rubies, and more. Anything you could possibly imagine."

"Interesting," Jourdan said, with a downward tick in his mouth.

"You are not convinced?" Lafitte asked.

Jourdan shrugged slightly. "Tell me more. I will not be held captive."

"You shall not," Lafitte said. "I will not bind and tie you like a rodent. If you turn over these two sapphires to me now, you shall be handsomely rewarded as well with every jewel you could desire. You shall want for nothing. Every nobleman in France shall be envious of you. Your reputation for wealth will last centuries. I would think two jewels now are a small price to pay for a lifetime of jewels."

"Why should I leave New Orleans? This is my home. I am well known here," Jourdan countered. "You are a pirate. Why should I trust a pirate?"

"Well played, Jourdan," Lafitte snickered. "Isla Mujeres is bigger and better than New Orleans."

Juliet stifled a reaction to Lafitte's lie.

He continued, "Isla Mujeres is a new location, has beautiful women, and all the rum you could want. It is paradise."

Pierre Jourdan wrinkled his nose at Lafitte. "Go on."

"The weather is perfect and there is no crime. You shall be a king among the natives. The women will love a classy Frenchman like yourself."

"That sounds promising to me."

"We are in agreement then?" Lafitte asked.

"Yes," Jourdan replied.

Lafitte held out his free hand and Jourdan shook it.

Internally, Juliet blew out a relieved sigh. She was thankful no swords were crossed nor ghost blood was shed. With the gentlemen's agreement sealed, Lafitte would keep all of the jewels in her hand, Pierre Jourdan would be going with Jean Lafitte back to Isla Mujeres, and The Lady of the Night and her entourage would get more tourists now that Jourdan would be gone. All would be happy.

Lafitte looked upward to the almost-full moon. He said to Jourdan, "Meet me back here once the moon has set and the sun has peaked over the horizon. We leave at dawn."

"I will be here. You may keep my two sapphires." With that, Pierre Jourdan handed his jewels to Juliet, turned on his heels, and disappeared into the night.

Turning to The Lady of the Night, Lafitte said, "Does that agreement meet your satisfaction? He has plans to travel with me tomorrow. You shall get what is coming to you."

She nodded and, for the first time, smiled at them.

Chapter 30

"That seemed a bit anticlimactic," Juliet said to Jean Lafitte as they headed back to Lafitte's Blacksmith Shop. The Lady of the Night and her ghostly gang had vaporized to their home bases. Compared to rowdy Bourbon Street, this part of The Quarter was quiet again.

"I was prepared to fight Jourdan, but I do not need to always plunder and pillage," Lafitte explained, tapping his sword secured at his sash, "but he was an amenable adversary and it did not take much to persuade him. A noble Frenchman like him is easily swayed by more money. Greed is a powerful curse."

Juliet nodded in agreement as they strolled northeast on Royal Street and made a left on Dumaine. The second-story balconies above them were lit up with jack-o' lanterns and orange string lights. Gauzy ghosts swayed in the late October breeze.

"Let me see the jewels," Lafitte said.

Reaching into her pocket, Juliet displayed the four gems in her palm. Lafitte picked each one up and examined them closely. "They are as I remember. Each facet is unblemished--even two hundred years later." He slipped them into a pocket inside his red velvet cloak.

"You don't want me to keep them?" Juliet asked.

"No, belle gosse. I am the one with the sword in case someone tries to take them from us."

"Fair enough." Juliet shrugged.

They made a right on Bourbon in front of Clover Grill. The 24/7 retro diner was full of patrons looking to fulfill their post-bar hopping munchies with burgers or all-day breakfast. The iconic restaurant even served as a movie scene in *The Curious Case of Benjamin Button* for Brad Pitt and Cate Blanchett in 2008.

They paused on the corner to allow a tour group to pass. At the helm, Adelaide caught Lafitte's eye and winked. The blue-haired tour guide never once broke in her banter of ghostly tales and legends that surrounded the city, adding an extra layer of mystique to the Halloween experience.

A minute later, they crossed the threshold into Lafitte's Blacksmith Shop. The tavern was filled with a late-night boisterous crowd, creating an atmosphere that buzzed with energy and excitement. The room was dimly lit, with warm golden hues emanating from the flickering candlelight that adorned the wooden tables scattered throughout the space.

The lack of electric lighting enhanced the feeling of stepping back in time. The air was thick with the scent of ale, but Juliet was used to it.

People in Halloween costumes gathered here, seeking respite from their daily routines. The crowd was a diverse tapestry, each individual bringing their own unique story and character to The Quarter. Men and women, young and old, mingled together, sharing laughter, conversation, and the occasional song from the piano. Twenty-somethings sat elbow-to-elbow with gray-haired grandmas belting out songs. A poster for the upcoming Halloween costume contest was plastered to the wall. Juliet couldn't wait to see what the holiday brought.

At the edge of it all stood the large, worn wooden bar, manned by Leah and Derek. They were skilled bartenders who swiftly poured frothy tankards of ale and filled glasses with Purple Drank. Patrons leaned against the bar, three-deep, eagerly awaiting their turn to be served. The clinking of glasses and the occasional cheer punctuated the constant hum of chatter that filled the room.

Leah caught Juliet's eye as she served a draft to a man in a zoo keeper costume. She waved her friend over as Derek joined them from the back room.

"Hey Jules, how'd it go?" Leah asked Juliet and Lafitte.

"We got the sapphires and the emeralds," Juliet said. She saddled up to the counter and Lafitte joined her.

"But no rubies," Lafitte sighed. "Alas, I do not know where they could be."

"And it looks like Marie Laveau won't make an appearance either," Juliet added.

"If I see her, I shall challenge her to a duel for double-crossing me," Lafitte sneered. "She must pay! I shall give her no mercy. She deserves the hangman's noose!"

"Y'all go all over The Quarter?" Derek asked as he popped the caps off of two bottles of Abita.

Lafitte nodded. "For as far as the shadows reached. We have come up empty." He shook his head. "If I do not find the rubies, my crew and I will be banished to *The Pride* for eternity. I have tasted being alive again thanks to this belle gosse--" He nodded to Juliet. "--and I cannot go back to purgatory."

Before Derek could respond, a couple of guys raised their voices in the corner. His bouncer instincts went on high alert.

"Watch yourself, asshole!" The taller one said to the other, scraping a wooden chair along the old floor.

The smaller one flew an insult back. Before fists clashed, Derek rushed over and separated the would-be prize fighters. "Break it up, fellas." He towered over both of them and made sure they took notice of his flexed biceps. The men staggered back and the taller one pressed his back against the wall near the portrait of Jean Lafitte.

Juliet and Lafitte watched quietly, hoping that neither would try to sucker punch the other. Thinking quickly, Juliet grabbed a bottle of water from the cooler and offered it to the man standing at the wall.

"Here," she said. "Take it easy." As he drank it and walked away, she pressed her hand against the brick wall. This was the same wall where she had previously seen the phantom red eyes. A few existing cracks spread along the brick wall and Juliet absently ran her fingers along them. Her hand snagged on a sharp edge and she inspected her fingers making sure she didn't cut herself. Instead, she found sandy debris with hints of minuscule pieces shining at her.

"What the hell?" she said to herself.

"What is it, belle gosse?" Lafitte asked. He peered over her shoulder and studied the small particles.

"This is usually where those phantom eyes linger in the corner," she said. A shudder ran through her body. "They creep me out. Thank god they aren't here now. But look at this." She held her sparkly dirt finger closer to Lafitte's face.

He sniffed it and wrinkled his nose. "It has an aroma of minerals and salt. Briny too. As if it was near the ocean."

"The Gulf is a hundred miles away."

"Aye." He smiled wide at her. "But I remember that scent."

He clawed at the wall, breaking away part of the centuries-old brick and cement.

Derek came running over. "What are you doin'? You're makin' a mess."

Lafitte ignored him, burrowing an inch into the infrastructure. He unsheathed his sword and dug further with the point. A small pile of shiny dirt and debris accumulated on the floor in front of them. Juliet, Derek, and Leah huddled around him, ignoring their customers.

Derek grabbed a candle from a nearby table and held it close to the hole in the wall. A glimmer of red peeked through a crevice.

"No way," they said in unison.

Carefully, Lafitte cautiously chipped away at the surrounding wall. Vivid red facets sparkled in front of them. He plucked a pair of rubies from the wall. The rubies he hadn't seen in two hundred years. The stunning and precious gems were rich in a blood-red color. Their warmth and energy captivated their small audience.

"They weren't phantom eyes after all," Juliet finally spoke. She had never seen anything so beautiful.

"I guess when a certain light hit that wall," Derek said, "it hit these rubies and they bounced back like they were ghostly eyes. No wonder the 'eyes' disappeared when the light moved. It all makes sense now."

"I wonder how long they've been there?" Leah asked. "How could we not know about this?"

Derek answered, "This buildin' is so old that they coulda been here for a hundred years and no one knew about them."

"You think Marie Laveau put them here?" Juliet asked. A V formed between her eyebrows. "A hundred fifty years ago?"

"'Tis possible," Lafitte said. "But it does not matter. I have them now. I have all of the jewels now." He dropped the rubies into his cloak pocket. "I can bring the treasure back to Isla Mujeres and my crew and I shall be free!"

Lafitte deposited the stones so quickly that Juliet didn't get a chance to react. Now that she had a moment to think, a mix of emotions filled her. She was thrilled that they found the jewels, and happy that Lafitte wouldn't be cursed to the Mississippi anymore. But her heart felt heavy. She knew he would be leaving the next day before the full moon came. He still had his arraignment in the morning, but after that, he would be gone. The past two weeks were an amazing adventure for her. She would never forget it.

Standing on a nearby table, Lafitte raised his sword. "We shall celebrate!" All of the customers in the room cheered and joined in the revelry. Hoots and hollers filled the tavern. Thirsty clientele moved en masse to the bar to order more drinks. Derek and Leah hurried back behind the counter trying to keep up. Knowing they were slammed, Juliet was torn between helping them and staying with Jean Lafitte. Her duty to serve drinks with them won out. "I can't party with you. Derek and Leah need my help. Are you staying here or what?"

"No, belle gosse," he said. "I shall return to *The Pride* and see my men."

"I get it." Juliet nodded quickly as more customers surrounded the bar to order drinks. "Just meet me at the courthouse tomorrow morning at 9:45. Don't forget."

"Aye." He tipped his chin at her.

Chapter 31

"Jean Lafitte!" A female voice bellowed from the shadows as he approached the docks of the Mississippi.

He jerked his head toward the unrecognizable sound. "Who is calling me? Show yourself."

"'Tis I," she yelled from the darkness. "The one whose curse you broke."

"Marie Laveau," he sneered, glancing side to side without seeing the voodoo queen. He raised his sword, prepared to fight.

"My contacts in the underworld have told me you have been snooping around my city." Her voice echoed into the night. "You came to my tomb. You swindled The Lady of the Night and Pierre Jourdan."

"I trusted you and you betrayed me."

She sniggered in the darkness.

"No one betrays Captain Jean Lafitte. Show yourself and fight." The notorious pirate who was feared across the

Caribbean swished his sword into a mist that formed around him. "Or are you a lily-livered coward?"

She laughed maniacally, her voice overpowering every other sound around them. "You fool! You may have broken my curse tonight, but you will not defeat me. I am the greatest voodoo queen of all eternity! Even in death, my followers still believe in me. Nothing can stop me."

"If you are the greatest as you say, then you shall have no fear in facing me." Lafitte held his ground on the sidewalk along the edge of The Quarter. "I look forward to being victorious over you, once and for all. You may have bested me once, but I do not intend to make that same mistake again. You have punished my crew and me long enough."

"Men are simpletons," she bellowed. "It will be easy to defeat you again." With that, the powerful voodoo priestess appeared in front of him, her eyes gleaming with a mixture of anger and determination. Her mystical reputation was whispered about in hushed tones across the city. Draped in dark robes adorned with intricate voodoo symbols, Marie chanted incantations that echoed through the swamps surrounding the city. She called upon the spirits of the waters and the ancient Creole, seeking their aid in her quest for revenge.

As the moon rose high in the night sky, a thick fog enveloped The Quarter, shrouding the pirate and the voodoo queen in an eerie mist.

Lafitte drew his cutlass and charged at Marie, thinking he could overpower her with brute force. But she raised her hands, and the waters of the nearby Mississippi River surged forth, forming a barrier that shielded her from his attack.

She laughed at him again, only fueling his desire for vengeance.

He lunged again. As his sword nicked her robe, she vanished from sight, only to appear ten feet away.

"You fool. You cannot defeat me," she taunted. With a voice that seemed to carry the weight of the spirits themselves, she held sway over mystical forces. "Those jewels are mine!"

Chants reverberated through the air as Marie called upon the vengeful spirits she had summoned. The elements seemed to obey her command, and a tempest brewed overhead. Lightning crackled.

Stopping, Lafitte closed his eyes and gathered his thoughts. His sword was not working against the powerful voodoo queen. He didn't have enough time to gather his crew to fight her. Nor did he know magic. Remembering what Madame Delia had told him, he had one other weapon in his artillery. Reaching into his pocket, he pulled only the rubies out and held them high. His arm shook as a feeling greater than himself took over. He wasn't sure what was about to happen, but he could feel power and protection.

"Those gemstones are mine!" she bellowed and lurched toward him.

"Not tonight!" He blocked her with his arm and she stumbled back.

Grumbling, Marie Laveau jerked toward Lafitte again, casting spells at him. Determination shone through her weathered features as she squared off against the pirate. Despite the passage of time leaving its mark on her, her eyes burned with an unyielding fire. Her wrinkled hands trembled as she raised them in a defensive posture, fingers curled into fists.

Lafitte held the rubies stiff-armed at Marie Laveau.

Her steps toward him were slow but deliberate, each movement calculated to conserve her energy.

Lafitte exuded confidence as he circled the old woman. He bounced lightly on the balls of his boots, his body ready to react to anything.

With a shriek, her final assault came with a vengeance. The wind swirled around her, casting debris into the air. Lightning filled the night. The ground shook and a nearby tree crumbled to the earth. She cast her hands toward him and colorful bolts of light came at him. Lafitte felt none of it, as if the rubies protected him.

"I told you you would not best me again," he sniggered.

"This is not over!" The defeated voodoo priestess snarled and vanished into the mists.

Chapter 32

With an ego full of victory, Lafitte made his way back to *The Pride*. His heeled boots made cadence on the Moonwalk Riverfront Park path. For almost two weeks, he knew his men had anxiously waited for his return. Together, they would make their way to Isla Mujeres with the jewels and bask in the island's tropics. He had defeated Marie Laveau but didn't want to risk testing the powerful jewels any longer.

Someone had left an empty dinghy tied to the river slip. Deftly, Lafitte untied it and rowed it to his ship.

Amidst the gentle currents of the Mississippi, the ship stood out against the serene backdrop - seemingly frozen in time. The ship's weathered wooden hull and masts evoked a sense of history and adventure. The crew was about to embark on their final quest. The ship's once-vibrant crimson and black sails hung limp, showing signs of wear and tear from the Gulf of Mexico elements.

Ronan, the quartermaster, an old man of ill repute, met Lafitte alone on the main deck. Ronan's black short jacket was now gray from the sun and river. His weathered face bore the marks of countless battles, with a rugged beard that flowed down to his chest, intertwined with beads and bits of shiny trinkets plundered from their conquests. The skin on his face was etched with wrinkles that told tales of a life lived on the edge of danger and adventure. Despite his grizzled appearance, it was his missing leg and eye that set him apart. His right leg had been replaced with a wooden peg, worn smooth from years of use. A patch covered his left eye socket.

Lafitte glanced around the empty ship. "Ronan, where are my men?" The silence surrounding *The Pride* was almost palpable, broken only by the distant sounds of water lapping against her sides and the occasional creak of wood as the ship shifted with the gentle flow of the river.

"Gone, Cap'n."

"What do you mean gone?" Lafitte gawked at empty hammocks swaying in the breeze. Weathered ropes dangled from the rigging, their frayed ends a testament to years of use and neglect. He strode to the abandoned ship wheel.

"They left, Cap'n." Trying to keep up with Lafitte, Ronan hobbled on his peg leg along the floorboards, making a popping sound. "When ye left at the new moon an' they saw nothin' happ'nd to ye in the river, they jumped overboard an' swam to shore."

"Putain!" Lafitte swore. "They abandoned me. They should have stayed focused on the journey's end." Lafitte then remembered what the bartender at MRB had said about seeing other pirates in The Quarter. And when strangers called him Jack Sparrow and mentioned the rest of his crew. He unsheathed his cutlass and raised it high. "If they come back, they shall be charged with mutiny."

"No, Cap'n." Ronan attempted to raise a hand to stop his leader, but thought twice about it. He didn't want to be charged with mutiny too. He had lived too long to spend his final days on the gallows. "They say they be back before the full moon. Say they wanted to crack Jenny's teacup and get loaded to the gunwales with grog."

"Hmph." Lafitte twirled his mustache between his fingers and stepped to the side of the ship. Before him, he could see crowds of partiers in the French Quarter. His crew was among them. "If they miss departure at sunrise, they may find themselves in Davy Jones' Locker." He knew the vibrant energy on Bourbon Street beckoned his band of pirates. In addition to the bars full of rum and loose women, he feared they'd get mesmerized by the snake charmers, drummers, and street performers.

"They promised they'd be back, Cap'n," Ronan said. "You see."

"If they are not here by dawn--" Lafitte gave a sly grin to his ailing quartermaster. "Then you shall be my new First Mate."

"Aye. Aye. Cap'n."

Chapter 33

The next morning, fighting through exhaustion because she had been slinging drinks until 2:00 a.m., Juliet paced the hall outside of Courtroom 1 at the Courthouse on Royal Street. Her heels clacked along the marble floor. Earlier that morning, she threw on a white blouse, a gray mini skirt, and heels instead of her usual rocker T-shirt and jeans for work. Her blonde hair was pulled back into a low ponytail. She hoped her conservative look would be in Jean Lafitte's favor with the judge. She checked the clock on her phone for the fifteenth time. 9:55.

"Where is he?" she sneered through gritted teeth. The hallway was empty except for a few staff members shuffling around from room to room.

The sound of footsteps coming closer around the corner caught Juliet's attention and she headed toward the sound.

"Where've you--" She came face to face with Officer Martinez and jumped when she bumped into him. "--been?"

Taking an embarrassed step back, Juliet grimaced and her cheeks burned crimson.

"I've been right here," he laughed.

"Sorry," she said, avoiding eye contact with him. "I thought you were someone else."

"I get that a lot," he laughed again. He towered over Juliet and she swooned momentarily at his muscles.

"I'm... I'm waiting for my friend." Juliet glanced over his shoulder to the empty hallway. "He was supposed to be here ten minutes ago. Hopefully, he's not passed out on Bourbon Street somewhere."

"The guy who thinks he's a pirate?" Officer Martinez asked.

"Yep. If he doesn't show, I'm out his bail money."

Officer Martinez reached into his pocket and handed her his card. "If he ditches you, give me a call. I might be able to do something. I need to cash in a few favors."

Juliet read his name out loud, "Eduardo Martinez."

He stared at her. "My friends call me Eddie. You can too." He took a step closer, but not too close so as not to invade her personal space. "If you like to get a cup of coffee sometime, let me know." His mouth formed a warm grin.

"I'd like that, Eddie." Juliet smiled back and held his card in her hand for a few extra seconds. Close up, she saw how cute he was. His brown eyes had flecks of gold in them and they glistened when he spoke to her. Juliet's heart thumped a few extra beats. Her cheeks flushed. "By the way, I like your ink." She pointed to his tattoo-filled bicep.

"Thanks." He dipped his chin toward her, taking away from his otherwise tough cop exterior.

Juliet took an extra second to gaze at him.

"Well, I gotta go," he said and glanced at the courtroom door. "And you do too."

"Crap!" Juliet shrieked and ran toward the doorway. She quickly turned back to him before disappearing into the room. "I'll text you!"

Inside the courtroom, Juliet found a seat at the defendant's table with an empty chair between her and the public defender. The old man wore a white linen suit with a blue tie that reminded her of Colonel Sanders. He probably smoked a cigar on the weekends with two fingers of brandy. "Good mornin', I'm Simon Thibeaux," he said, his deep southern drawl coming through. "I'll represent the client. Is he comin'?"

"I hope so," Juliet said. She turned back to the empty doorway and shrugged.

"He's got about another minute 'til the judge comes in."

The paneled walls gleamed with polished wood. The district attorney waited at the table across the aisle. A bailiff stood at attention near the state and national flag poles. A large seal of Louisiana was displayed behind the bench. The court reporter sat at a small desk. A mixture of pine cleaner and stale air filled the room.

The sight of the empty seat next to her filled Juliet with anger. Under the table, she held clenched fists in her lap and she swore she could feel steam escaping her ears. "Damn him," she cussed under her breath.

A moment later, in long black robes, a female judge entered the room through a paneled door.

"All rise," the bailiff directed and everyone stood. "Judge Nannette Triche Barbier residing."

Judge Barbier was a 50-ish Black woman who commanded the room. "Please be seated." When everyone in the room sat back down, she spoke again. "Mr. Thibeaux, it appears that your client is not here."

"That is correct." The public defender stood and shrugged.

"His charges are public urination, resisting arrest, stealing a horse, and assault with a deadly weapon."

"Yes, ma'am."

Beside him, a tightness filled Juliet but she held her composure. She wanted to punch Jean Lafitte for not showing up. The usually-successful pirate didn't stand a chance with her.

The judge spoke again, "Since the defendant is not here, a bench warrant will be issued for his arrest and the case will proceed in his absence." She turned to Juliet. "Ms. Vance, your friend didn't show up. His behavior is inexcusable. That said, I'm sorry but your bail money will be forfeited."

A hard pit formed in Juliet's stomach. She suppressed a scream that gurgled inside her. The whites of her eyes dominated her face. She swallowed hard and finally answered the judge. "Okay," was all she could utter.

"A trial will be scheduled for thirty days from now." Judge Barbier raised her gavel and pounded it down. She stood and disappeared through the same paneled door.

A few minutes later, Juliet stomped through the hallway of the courthouse. How could she have been so stupid? Jean Lafitte was a pirate! A lying, cheating, thieving pirate! Not only did he lie to Pierre Jourdan and The Lady of the Night, but he lied to her, too. He promised her multiple times he would show up. She hated herself for trusting him. It was her own fault for being so naive. She was out $700 and would never see it again. This was worse than getting fired from Willa Jean. She never should have given Lafitte the jewels. She should have held onto them as insurance for him to show up to his arraignment. Juliet couldn't believe Lafitte stiffed her!

Seething, Juliet slammed through the courthouse doors and clomped onto the sidewalk. She spat out, "If I ever see him again, I swear I'll kill him! Even if I have to conjure up Marie Laveau to do it!"

Chapter 34

When Juliet got home, her anger hadn't subsided. Everyone she passed on the sidewalk gave her a wide berth on the sidewalk and didn't want to be subject to her wrath. The normally quiet Marigny neighborhood had its own personal hurricane. She didn't even bother saying hello to Mrs. Hebert next door.

In her kitchen, Juliet pulled out her phone and called Leah. "Have you seen Laffite?"

"No, why?"

"Because the douche-bag didn't show up for his arraignment this morning and I lost seven hundred dollars!"

"I haven't seen him since he left the tavern last night. Sorry."

"Well, if you see him, let me know, and I'll be right there. He'll have a lot more to worry about than a voodoo curse!"

Juliet hung up with Leah and called Derek. Steam puffed out of her nose. She wanted to hurl something out her window.

"Hello?" Derek groggily said into the phone.

"Oh. So sorry to wake you."

"It's cool. The twins have been up for a coupla hours now. I think I finally got them to settle down. What's up?"

"Have you seen Lafitte? He bailed on me this morning."

"No, sorry."

"It's okay. I'll find him. Take care of those babies."

Juliet ended the call with Derek and angrily pulled baking supplies out of her cabinets, slamming doors in her wake. Baking something would calm her. Otherwise, a random stranger might be on the receiving end of her wrath. She didn't have the patience right now to wait for pecan pie to bake, so Bananas Foster was on the menu. A few swigs of rum wouldn't hurt either. After the morning she had, she deserved it.

After melting butter in a skillet, Juliet stirred in brown sugar and cinnamon. Bananas Foster was a favorite guilty pleasure and, hopefully, it would soothe her. She considered herself a good pâtissier, but she could never do it exactly how it was made at Brennan's Restaurant, the famous pink restaurant on Royal Street, where the scrumptious dessert originated. Juliet stirred in banana liqueur and placed the bananas in the pan. After taking a few swallows herself, she added rum and let it simmer. She grabbed a candle lighter and ignited the rum.

For a few moments, the blue and orange flame left Juliet mesmerized and a small feeling of calmness filled her. She was still furious with Jean Lafitte but she swore to leave no collateral damage.

Grabbing a scoop of vanilla ice cream, Juliet slid the bananas onto it and spooned her sauce over top. The scrumptious treat helped decrease her heart rate. She went outside to her back patio with the dessert in hand to enjoy the late October warm weather. Before she could sit down, she noticed something on her metal table. Jean Lafitte's gold-handled sword sparkled in the midday sun.

"What the--" Juliet inched over to it. The sword lay on top of a note and Juliet snatched it up.

She read:

My dear belle gosse,   27 October 2023

Regretfully, I could not attend the arraignment this morning. You have my deepest apologies if this put you in dire financial straits. With the full moon approaching tomorrow night, I must leave with my crew to Isla

Mujeres to return the cursed jewels. My destiny depends on it.

Pierre Jourdan was not welcome on my ship, after all. He was an unworthy adversary when he double-crossed me and led us astray to find the sapphires at the antique shop. Hence, he shall remain at Muriel's for eternity.

Consequently, The Lady of the Night and the rest of her cohorts shall not gain more visitors as she requested. She was also not worthy. And so, the status quo remains.

But you, belle gosse, you are worthy. I must apologize for departing without saying goodbye, but I must be on my way before the full moon arrives. You have been nothing but kind and accepting of me, despite your early hesitance. I leave you my precious sword, as you deserve it. Take it to Roberta at the antique shop and you shall receive a king's ransom. The coinage should be more than enough to cover your financial situation and then some.

Farewell, belle gosse.

Until we meet again.

Captain Jean Lafitte

The heavy gold-handled sword weighed down Juliet's hand. The rake was genuine after all. She muttered under her breath, "Son of a bitch…"

Chapter 35

As the full moon ascended the next night, *The Pride* and her crew dropped anchor just off the southern coast of Isla Mujeres, on the quiet side, away from the noise. In the near darkness, turquoise waters rippled at the edge of the ship. At her helm, Jean Lafitte held the tropical island's precious gems in his cloak pocket. The curse was near completion and he had waited long enough to enjoy the rest of his bountiful life. He wasn't sure how long he had left, but now he had the freedom to do what he wished. The now empty space on his sash where his sword had hung was foreign to him. But he knew the priceless piece was in good hands. He would miss Juliet.

Two hundred years earlier, he and his men arrived on the sandy white shores of Isla Mujeres, looking for a slower pace after months of marauding on the Caribbean Sea. The island's strategic location plus the protective waters of Laguna Makax made a perfect refuge for his buccaneers. The Spanish transported massive amounts of gold from the Yucatan to

Europe and he and his band of pirates took advantage of the opportunity to blunder the merchant ships.

On his last trip, the island's priestess Paloma agreed to allow Lafitte to keep his base on the island. Paloma was a direct descendant of the goddess Ixchel. The island served as the sanctuary for Ixchel, the Mayan goddess of happiness, fertility, medicine, and the moon. The moon. Lafitte lived and died by the moon.

Paloma had warned Lafitte of her jewels' special powers: to curse men for 200 years and to bring women to their greatest dominance. No wonder Marie Laveau stole them. The priestess had cautioned Lafitte and his men to never remove the jewels from the island. If only Cedric the Gunner had listened. He succumbed to the gems' brilliance and paid the ultimate price. Now Lafitte and his men's purgatory debt would finally end.

The Pride's crew gathered on the ship's deck in front of Lafitte, their eagerness consumed them. The quartermaster, his one eye covered with a patch, held his head up and alert. The boatswain chewed his bottom lip, or what was left of it. The rest of the ragtag crew leaned forward, waiting for direction. Their livelihoods were in Lafitte's hands.

"Avast ye mateys," Lafitte shouted to them, "the time is now!"

Cheers erupted in front of him. The men hoisted steins of grog in salute. Lafitte reached into his pocket and raised the six precious cursed jewels to his men. Their brilliance sparkled under the full moon's light.

"Our destiny awaits!" Lafitte yelled. More cheers roared from the crew. "We lost a few men to the pleasures of Bourbon Street, but the rest of us shall persevere! Move on!"

Leaving their captain, the pirates scrambled over each other racing and swimming to the water's edge toward land. Many fell to the sand, rubbing it over them as if it was the massive gold treasure that Edmond Dantès recovered in *The Count of Monte Cristo*. The air carried a warm, balmy breeze, laden with the scents of saltwater and exotic flowers, inviting them to explore the mystique that unfolded. The soft, powdery sand stretched out before them, illuminated by the moonlight's gentle glow. The beach was devoid of footprints, offering an untouched ambiance that resonated with tranquility.

The men basked in the moonlight, laughing and joking, as their captain departed his dinghy and stood above them. Lafitte's gaze pointed upward. The night sky revealed its brilliance, scattered with countless stars that twinkled like diamonds against a black velvet canvas. The moon, in its full glory, cast a radiant glow upon the landscape, bathing everything in a silver sheen. Its reflection shimmered on the calm waters, creating a pathway of ethereal light that led to distant horizons. The moon that once was an enemy was now an alliance.

"We are here, men," he mused. "We have arrived." A small smile of hope formed on his lips. The jewels in his fist were finally home.

The atmosphere was alive with a sense of peace. Except for his men, the absence of other humans allowed Lafitte to immerse himself fully in the moment, appreciating the beauty of nature's nocturnal marvels. He reflected on the last time he was on the island.

Along the shoreline, towering palm trees swayed gently in the breeze, their leaves whispering secrets in hushed tones. The rustling of their fronds created a soothing melody, and their silhouettes danced against the night sky, casting intricate patterns of shadow and light.

As Lafitte approached the palms, a young woman in a pink and blue flowered sarong emerged from the jungle. Her dark hair was piled high on her head. A red hibiscus bloom was tucked behind her ear.

"Captain Lafitte," she purred. "I have been waiting for your arrival." She gestured to the full moon, her skin shimmering beneath its light.

"Who are you?" he wanted to know. She reminded him of someone he met long ago on the island.

She ignored his question and said, "The island stones were taken and I must ensure their safe return. I can only assume you have them since you are here."

"Aye." He nodded slightly to her and opened his fist. The gems' captivating brilliance fascinated him. Their dazzling display of colors and radiance sparkled in the night.

"Good," she said. "Follow me." She turned and disappeared into the foliage.

Leaving his men behind to enjoy their freedom, Lafitte followed her along a forest path. As darkness blanketed the island, a symphony of sounds emerged from every corner. The rhythmic chorus of insects resonated through the air, accompanied by the distant calls of nocturnal creatures. The atmosphere was thick with humidity, carrying scents of damp earth, rich vegetation, and blooming flowers.

Beneath the canopy, the palms stretched upwards, their towering forms cloaked in shadows. Moonlight filtered through the gaps in the foliage, casting ethereal beams upon the island floor. The leaves, now a deeper shade of green, rustled gently beneath Lafitte's boots.

The young woman led him to an open area where they approached a decrepit altar. The solemn, ancient structure was made of solid, weathered stone, bearing the marks of time and the weight of Mayan history. Standing as a testament to the passage of ages, the old altar exuded an aura of reverence and mystery. Its massive form, crafted from rough-hewn stone, commanded attention and respect. She knelt before the sacred space.

Without facing him, she said, "This is where the jewels belong for eternity. Paloma watched over them until your men stole them from her." She turned back to him. "You and your men have paid your debt for the past two centuries." She held an open hand to him.

Without a word, Lafitte gently dropped the rubies, sapphires, and emeralds in her palm. She placed the precious gems on top of the altar. The broad, flat surface had witnessed countless ceremonies, bearing the weight of sacrificial objects, incense, and sacred texts. It bore faded Mayan inscriptions and symbols, their original meanings lost to the annals of history.

Above, the night sky unveiled its celestial wonders. Stars twinkled brightly, unobstructed by artificial lights. The constellations appeared vivid and clear, their patterns etched against the vast canvas of the heavens. The moon cast an ethereal glow, enhancing the mystique of the sacred altar.

"Now that the jewels have been returned, what shall become of me and my men?" Lafitte asked.

The woman smiled warmly and stood. "You have two choices. Like your thief had two choices. He did not choose wisely."

"What are my choices?"

"If you leave the island, you are at the mercy of mortality."

"And if we do not?" He arched an eyebrow at her.

"If you choose to stay here, time does not exist on this side of the island." She gestured toward their tropical surroundings.

"You will be like me. I do not age. The jewels granted me extraordinary powers."

"And you are?" He stared at her. "You did not state your name earlier."

"Paloma."

Chapter 36

Three months later

Juliet paced back and forth along the royal blue and white checkered tile floor. She nervously bit her lip for the hundredth time. She checked and rechecked a large display counter showcasing an enticing array of pecan pralines, turtle cheesecake, bourbon balls, and her famous bread pudding. At the far end, her opus, a gold, green, and purple King Cake, sparkled with candied sugar, stood ready for Carnival. Along the white brick wall, a giant chalkboard announced in ruby-red lettering daily specials of Mardi Gras lemon bark, sweet potato pie, and bourbon bacon brittle.

The floor was scrubbed. The matching bathroom was spotless. Sapphire-blue waxy to-go bags were stacked and ready. The sweet mixture of sugar, coffee, and chocolate filled the air.

Everything had to be perfect. Juliet had learned the art of baking from her mother, and she poured her passion into every creation. Excitement filled her stomach and she was finally ready. She wiped her hands on her apron and admired her work. This was go-time.

Mardi Gras was still a month away, but the city was already in full swing. Private social clubs hosted extravagant balls. Krewes had collected beads, plastic doubloons, stuffed animals, and other "throws" for the past several months to bestow upon parade-goers as their floats, marching bands, costumed dancers, and their own royalty strutted down St. Charles Avenue. Elaborate masks covered the faces of reality beneath a deep and colorful veil. Delectable indulgences of every kind were realized before they had to be discreetly tucked away during Lent, a time of penance. Deep pagan roots and profound class divisions lay at the heart of the jubilant season. The city overflowed with tourists and locals alike. Gold, purple, and green reigned supreme and adorned decorations on every door and balcony of the French Quarter and adjacent neighborhoods. Parades traveled through the entire city for two weeks.

The bell on the door jingled, jerking Juliet out of her thoughts.

"Hey babe," Eddie said. He was dressed in his dark blue police uniform. "I wanted to stop by and wish you good luck before I go on duty." He kissed her on the mouth. "You'll do great. I know it." After spending hours talking at Café Du Monde and a scrumptious dinner at Antoine's complete with Baked Alaska, Juliet's dry streak of dating came to an end. She told Eddie the whole story about her adventure with Jean Lafitte and her ability to see the spirits of the city. Now that Lafitte was gone, so was her power. She thought for sure she had scared Eddie off and he would ghost her. To her surprise, he was intrigued by her tale and wanted to learn more about her.

Since Lafitte failed to show up for his hearing, Eddie had explained to Juliet that the NOPD kept Lafitte's pistol that they had confiscated when Lafitte was arrested. The department had it appraised, and, to their surprise, the gun was valued at $400,000. The officers used the money to buy some new squad cars, more horses to add to their team, and remodeled parts of the precinct.

"Thanks, sweetie. Derek and Leah texted me good luck too. They'll stop by later."

"I gotta go catch some bad guys. Maybe I'll get lucky this time and won't take a bottle to the face." He ran his finger along a new scar that formed along his right cheek.

"Don't you know that chicks dig scars?" Juliet reached up and kissed his new wound. She was thrilled Eddie was hot *and* sweet. He had no idea how cute he was.

"Okay, babe, I'll see ya later." Eddie left Juliet in the 1880s-era building that she bought deep in the heart of the

Marigny. The neighborhood was home to some of New Orleans' trendiest restaurants, art galleries, and antique stores that offered unique items for every pocketbook, from museum-quality art to thrift-shop chic. Juliet was now one of them.

Three months earlier, when Jean Lafitte bequeathed his sword to her, she heeded his advice and brought the prized weapon to Keil's Antiques. Roberta appraised the sword for over a million dollars. Collectors were willing to pay the hefty price tag. Upon hearing the exorbitant amount, Juliet felt drunk with joy. She immediately paid off the credit card that she used for the pirate's bail money and all of the other money she had incurred since she met him. After a few days of discussing options with Leah and Derek, she bought the commercial building a few blocks from her house. It was opening day.

With one final deep breath garnering all the courage she could muster, Juliet flipped the emerald-green sign on the glass door: "Jewels Bakery. Open!"

The End

Thank you for reading my book.

If you enjoyed it, won't you please take a moment to leave me a review at your favorite retailer?

One or two sentences are perfectly fine.

Thanks!

Want some cool merch from me?

Post a pic of this book on your social media and tag me!

@marywalshwrites

Tag me on:

Order autographed books at:

marywalshwrites.com

Follow me on Goodreads and Amazon:

www.goodreads.com/goodreadscommarywalshwrites

www.amazon.com/author/marywalsh2